Dear Reader,

Love at first sight can be a dream come true, but sometimes second chances can be even sweeter. This month, four breathtaking new romances from Bouquet prove it!

Veteran author Colleen Faulkner starts us off with the first in the new Bachelors Inc. miniseries, **Marrying Owen,** the story of an estranged couple forced into close quarters by a sudden storm—and ready to give love another try. Next up is the final installment in Vivian Leiber's the Men of Sugar Mountain trilogy, **Three Wishes.** When a man from her past returns to her small town, one woman wonders if he's now the key to the future she's always hoped for.

Sometimes romance blooms in the most unexpected places. That's what happens when the heroine of Wendy Morgan's **Ask Me Again** finds herself in a wedding party with the most boring guy she knew in college—and discovers he's become a fascinating and sexy man. Finally, Susan Hardy proves that every cloud really does have a **Silver Lining** when an accident that threatens everything one woman has leads her into the arms of a man who becomes the one thing she really wants.

Laughter, tears, desire, and most of all, love—Bouquet delivers them all. Why not give one a chance today?

Kate Duffy
Editorial Director

UP A TREE

"How's it going?" Tom asked.

Dorothy swung her feet back and forth. "Oh, can't complain." She made no move to jump down, but continued to swing her legs as if she were relaxing on a porch swing rather than stuck up a tree. She liked this perspective on things. Usually, she had to look up at *him*. Through the loose-fitting neck of his cotton shirt, she could see the outline of his pectoral muscles with their mat of crisp, springy, black hair. Her mouth watered, and it wasn't from the sour apple she'd just eaten. Despite the interesting view, Dorothy was suddenly struck by the urge to be on the ground beside him.

"Would you help me down?" she said.

"I thought you'd never ask."

He stepped closer and reached both arms up to her. As she slid off the branch, he lifted her gently into his powerful arms and let her settle against his chest. Her arms slid naturally along his until they came to rest on his shoulders. Her cheek lay against his chest, and she could hear his heart beating like a trip-hammer. Or was it her own?

Were her feet really touching the ground? Was that really his mouth brushing the top of her head with a kiss?

Instead of letting her go, he tightened his arms around her and pressed a soft, sweet kiss to her neck. A jolt went through her and her knees buckled.

For a moment she was afraid he would let her go, but instead he ran his hand along her cheek and cupped her chin, then tipped her head up and brought his face close to hers, bringing his lips down on hers in a searing kiss. . . .

SILVER LINING

Susan Hardy

Zebra Books
Kensington Publishing Corp.
http://www.zebrabooks.com

ZEBRA BOOKS are published by

Kensington Publishing Corp.
850 Third Avenue
New York, NY 10022

First Printing: August, 2000
10 9 8 7 6 5 4 3 2 1

Printed in the United States of America

This book is dedicated, with loving thanks, to all my critique partners: Melissa Beck, Jacquie D'Alessandro, Marge Gargosh, Carina Rock, Carol Springston, Lynn Styles, Pat Van Wie, and especially my main mentor, Donna Sterling.

One

Katherine Spencer struggled with the heavy rope that bound her hands behind her back. The nylon bit painfully into her wrists, but she persisted—escape was her only chance.

Finally she was able to reach the knot with her fingertips, wishing she had let herself be talked into that set of extra-long "glamour" nails her manicurist liked so much. Then she might have more leverage at least. Good thing the bad guys tied lousy knots. If there was one thing her sailing enthusiast father had taught her—actually, the *only* thing she could remember him taking the time to teach her—it was how to tie a good knot.

During her ride from the university, bound and gagged and bouncing in the trunk of a rusted-out hunk of junk with bad shocks, she'd had plenty of time to think about how this kidnapping scenario would likely play out.

She knew she would be held for ransom. The bumbling pair of kidnappers had the courtesy to tell her that much as they trussed her up. The bad guys had done their homework—up to a point. Just finding out what she looked like must have been a deceptively difficult thing. If her jet-setting parents had done one thing right, it was keeping her out of the spotlight growing up. She didn't think a photo of her had ever appeared in a consumer publication. But the kidnappers hadn't gone far enough in their research. If they'd known a little more about her, they'd have realized the flaw in their plan.

No ransom would be paid for Katherine Spencer.

The man the kidnappers were planning to approach for her ransom was no longer her fiancé. Hours before her abduction, she'd given him back his ring, and he'd flown into a rage. He wouldn't pay her ransom from his fortune. Neither would the ransom be paid from her inheritance. Her late parents' lawyers and accountants would follow standard police procedure and refuse to pay on principle.

When her kidnappers realized she was worthless . . . A chill came over her, threatening to throw the straining muscles of her arms and back into spasms. As she tried to relax for a moment, she cheered herself with a more positive thought. The bad guys had made two other mistakes, and these were in *her* favor.

Mistake number one—beside the dingy mattress where she'd been unceremoniously dumped, there was a window. And it was open. A flimsy screen and about a six-foot drop to the ground were all that lay between her and freedom. Mistake number two—and this was the real beaut—as they'd dragged her out of the trunk and slammed it behind her, they'd left the keys in the lock.

She had to get to that car before they realized the keys were missing. She went at the knot again with renewed vigor. It was hard to believe that only a few hours ago she'd been having a great time at a bon voyage party thrown in her honor. She'd finally mustered the courage to break up with Michael, and was looking forward to her summer sabbatical away from her job as a professor and child psychologist.

She'd meant to arrange for time off long before this, but her cases kept getting in the way. It seemed that every time she would think of going on a holiday, one of her patients would reach some critical stage of treatment. How could she let down the trusting children who depended on her?

She'd finally managed to get some time off, promising herself not to think about work for a while. She didn't even tell her friends, coworkers, or household staff where she was going. She should have at least told Matty and Jacob, her family's cook and groom, who'd been like parents to her for so many years, but when she spoke to them last, she hadn't decided where she was going. She had decided to be impulsive for once in her life, and look where it had gotten her. "See you in the fall," was all she'd said to her friends as she left the party.

Katherine continued to loosen the knot until she felt it coming apart, and she tasted the faint coppery taste that accompanies an adrenaline surge. When her hands were finally free of the ropes, she quickly untied the bandanna gagging her and bent to undo the rope binding her ankles.

When her legs were free, she leapt to her feet and tiptoed to the window. She pushed gingerly at the screen, hoping she could dislodge it without making much noise. Her luck held. The screen came loose at the bottom, swinging outward noiselessly just enough for her to squeeze through. She doffed her pumps, stowing them under her arm, and pushed through the window, landing safely on the grass below.

Katherine carefully edged around the house and saw the old Cadillac. The box of bolts, with its shiny keys still in the trunk lock, now looked like the chariot of the gods. She tiptoed toward the Caddy, trying not to make crunching noises on the gravel. Katherine ducked as she passed the living room window, where she heard the low drone of the TV and what she hoped was snoring from at least one of the kidnappers.

When she reached the car, she slid the keys out of the trunk lock and opened the driver's door. Once inside, she pulled the door closed with nothing more than a gentle click and locked all four doors. Throwing her shoes on the floorboard, she put the key into the ignition. "Lord, thanks for letting me get this far. Now, please let this buggy start."

It did. Throwing the car into reverse, she cut the wheel hard toward the house until she had the clearance she needed. Just as she shifted into drive, she looked in the rearview mirror to see the kidnappers tumbling out of the house, tripping over each other as they ran.

Stamping hard on the accelerator with her bare foot, she rained a shower of gravel on her hapless former captors and roared down the driveway. She whooped as she cranked down the window. Thrusting out her arm, she gave the kidnappers an appropriate good-bye salute. "Just a little token of my esteem, boys!"

On the overnight trip to this godforsaken place, she'd

made a mental note of the direction of turns they had taken once they had left the main road and gotten onto this bone-rattling dirt one. She turned right and headed for the highway. Although the Kansas sky up ahead was a threatening yellowish gray, she didn't care. She was free.

"Faster! Faster, Daddy! The tornado's gaining on us!"

Tom Weaver checked the funnel cloud in the rearview mirror for what must have been the hundredth time in the last five minutes. Jamey was right. It *was* gaining on them.

The twister reached down out of the sky in a jagged gray column of whirling dust and debris. Vivid shards of lightning illuminated the deadly storm, bringing it into sharp, horrifying focus. A bolt of pure panic shot through him. He started to swear, but the words died on his lips. He didn't want the last words his son heard from him to be profanity.

He glanced down quickly at Jamey. The boy was clearly terrified. Tom wished there was something he could say to comfort his son, but even though he was only five, Jamey knew exactly how much trouble they were in.

He looked in the mirror again and gritted his teeth. The damned thing was closer even though he was practically standing on the accelerator. If they could just make it to that overpass up ahead, they might have a chance.

"Is the tornado going to set a house on us like in

The Wizard of Oz?" Jamey looked up at him with trusting eyes.

"No, son," Tom said, not at all sure that the twister wouldn't do just that, even though this stretch of road cut through mostly farmland with few houses close by.

He'd begun to regret buying Jamey that *Wizard of Oz* video. He must have watched it a hundred times. He'd have to have a talk with his son about his television viewing habits—that is, if they lived to see tomorrow.

Up ahead, the sky was overcast but tranquil. Safety, in the form of the Roberts Road overpass, was a hundred yards away. The rearview mirror reflected the evil yellow-purple colors of a killer storm. His mind refused to judge the distance between the truck and the twister.

By the time they reached the overpass, Tom had stopped looking back, but as soon as he'd killed the engine, the storm's awful roar became deafening. As he jumped from the truck and slung Jamey over his shoulder, he thought absurdly of every poor bastard he'd ever seen on the nightly news in the wake of one of these storms. With a microphone shoved into a face gone ashen with shock, the fellow always said, "It sounded like a freight train." And so it did.

The rain-soaked grass of the roadside was so slippery he almost fell, but once he reached the rough concrete, his heavy work boots gained some traction. The wind plucked at the back of his denim jacket as if to pull him toward the storm, but he fought forward, racing up the man-made hill that supported the overpass and reaching the top in seconds. He wedged himself as tightly as possible into the angle formed by the concrete hill and the road up above and folded himself over his sobbing son's small body.

The tornado was upon them now, but they were as safe as they were going to be, so he dared to open his eyes. The screaming demon of a twister seemed to lose its form as it approached, then went over them, whipping the tall grass furiously as it did. When it continued on its path down the highway, it resumed its shape and form.

Heaving a sigh of relief, Tom relaxed and allowed Jamey to wriggle from his grasp. They watched the departing tornado in awed silence. Then Tom saw something that made his blood run cold once more. A car he hadn't seen before, coming from the direction they'd been headed, was trying to turn around in the roadway. It was too late for the driver to make a dive for the ditch on the side of the road. The twister was headed straight for the car.

Tom swallowed hard. *You'll never make it,* he thought.

The tornado seized the car and dribbled it along the pavement like a basketball.

"Look, Dad! Look at that!" Jamey stabbed a chubby forefinger in the direction of the car.

"I see it." Tom winced as the twister dashed the car to the ground one last time, like a disgusted child casting aside a broken toy. Then it moved on. "Let's go." Tom took Jamey's hand and they ran for the truck.

As he started the engine, Tom looked down at Jamey. Tom wouldn't have subjected his son to any unpleasantness or trauma for all the corn in Kansas, but he had no choice. He had to check on that driver, or what was left of him.

They reached the car in seconds. When Jamey went for the door handle, Tom stopped him. "No, Jamey. You have to stay here."

"But Dad!" the child began in a howl of protest. "I want to go too!"

"No way. I mean it. Stay put right here until I come back."

Tom headed for the car, steeling himself for what he might find. It was an old, powder blue Cadillac unless he missed his guess, or had been until the twister turned it into something that looked more like an accordion. Thank God it was right-side up at least.

As he came to the driver's side, his breath caught. A woman, still belted into her seat, sprawled forward awkwardly over the wheel. A profusion of long brown hair obscured her face.

He didn't know enough about first aid to try and move the woman himself, so he decided to call for help from his cellular phone. When he called, they would probably want him to provide some idea of her condition.

Gingerly, he reached through the driver's open window. First, he had to move aside that cascading mane of hair to reach her throat. When his fingertips made contact with the soft silky stuff, he jerked back his hand as if he'd been burned. This woman was alive all right. He couldn't have said why, but he knew this instinctively, even though he hadn't actually felt her pulse.

Through his work-roughened skin, the feel of this

anonymous woman's hair brought up a wellspring of un-bidden emotions, not all of them pleasant. Had it really been that long since he'd touched a woman's hair? He cursed himself. This woman obviously needed help, and he was behaving like an idiot.

He tried again, brushing her hair aside until he was touching her throat. He tried to ignore the satiny smooth texture of her skin as he felt for a pulse. Closing his eyes to aid his concentration only heightened the aware-ness of her softness, her warmth, the suppleness of her flesh as his fingers felt their way blindly across it. It was as if he felt her skin not just on the surface of his calloused fingers, but in his blood and bones.

He felt it then, weak but steady. Her heartbeat thrummed against his fingertips.

He uttered a simple prayer of gratitude as he ran back to the truck. He slid into the cab and dialed the cellular phone, holding up a hand to silence an avalanche of questions from Jamey.

"Carl Meadows." The emergency medical technician stationed at the local firehouse identified himself, his voice crackling with storm-induced static.

"Carl, it's Tom Weaver. I'm out on Route 10 near the Roberts Road overpass. A twister just went by and tossed a car around some. There's a woman inside, alive but unconscious."

"We'll be right there."

Tom returned to the car to wait for the ambulance. He kept a close eye on the woman, but she didn't stir. Why hadn't he ever taken any first aid courses? He hated the feeling of helplessness, the feeling that noth-ing he could do would make any difference. He hadn't had that feeling since his marriage had started to crumble.

The breakup had been like a freight train bearing down on him. He knew it was coming, but he'd been powerless to stop it. At first he thought he'd be able to help his wife solve her problems by using all the kindness he possessed plus the sheer force of his will. But he'd only ended up being as helpless as he felt right now.

Although it seemed to Tom like hours, the ambulance was there within minutes. Carl and his partner Lonny jumped from the vehicle and went to the car.

Tom felt something touch his leg and turned around to see Jamey standing behind him. "I thought I told you to stay in the truck."

Jamey planted his feet shoulder-width apart and set his fists on his hips, a sure sign that he meant to stand his ground. "You said to stay in the truck until you came back, and then you came back, you didn't say anything about what I should do after that."

Tom opened his mouth to correct his son's fuzzy, five-year-old logic, but Carl cut him off.

"You and Jamey okay, Tom?" He was removing a stretcher from the back of the ambulance.

"Yeah, fine. It was close, but we made it to the overpass. The woman in the Caddy wasn't so lucky."

Tom helped Carl and Lonny open the damaged car door to begin their preliminary examination of the woman.

"Is she going to be okay, Dad?"

Tom put his hand on his son's small shoulder. "I don't know. But I'm sure Carl and Lonny are going to do their best." He looked at the boy's solemn little face. At this point, Jamey might as well stay.

In a few minutes Carl and Lonny had carefully placed the woman on the stretcher. Under the red jacket she wore a fancy black dress, cut well above the knee. She was tall, slender but curvy in all the right places, and shoeless. Her luxuriant hair, in wild disarray, still covered her face. Tom felt himself longing to see the face that hid behind that riot of beautiful hair.

He watched the regular rise and fall of her breasts as if in a trance. In fact, the whole scene had taken on a surreal quality. He, Jamey, and the other men were like four of the Seven Dwarfs clustered around Snow White, waiting for her to wake up.

As Lonny applied a blood pressure cuff to her upper arm, Carl gently guided layers of hair away from her face. Then he moved away, giving Tom a clear view of the mysterious Caddy driver. Besides the ugly purple bruise on her forehead, she looked fine. Well, more than fine, actually, Tom allowed. In fact, she was beautiful. The bruise was the only flaw in an otherwise perfect oval face. Thick lashes curled against her rosy cheeks. Her skin was like porcelain and her generous, slightly pouty lips were the stuff of men's dreams.

Open your eyes, he pleaded silently.

She did.

As if on cue, the sun came out, and their surroundings went from stormy sepia tones to Technicolor all in one blink of her electric blue eyes. Tom exhaled sharply, only now aware that he'd been holding his breath. The grass looked greener and the poppies blooming along the roadside seemed redder.

Carl and Lonny began a litany of questions. What year was it? Who was the President? What town was she in? Could she move her hands and feet? In a shaky voice, she obediently murmured satisfactory responses to some questions, but was undecided on others. The two technicians exchanged concerned glances.

"That's just fine," Carl said soothingly. "Now, tell us your name."

The woman blinked her long lashes and her eyebrows drew together in concentration. Then her perfect, Cupid's bow lips tried to form a word, or a name, but nothing came out.

"Who are you, lady?" Lonny repeated gently. "What's your name?"

The woman studied the faces of the men surrounding her, then blinked again. "I don't know."

There was a moment of silence and then Tom realized that Jamey had pushed past him to stand at the woman's side. He carried a red high-heeled shoe in each hand.

"Dorothy!"

Carl and Lonny turned to look at the little boy. The injured woman stared at Jamey hopefully, as if perhaps he knew who she was.

"Jamey," Tom began. "Don't start . . ."

The child ignored him. "It's just like in the movie. The tornado picked her up and set her back down and she had a bump on her head. It's Dorothy! I even found her ruby slippers!" Jamey held up the red snakeskin shoes triumphantly.

"Jamey! Why did you go in that car? You could have been cut by broken glass."

Jamey shrugged. Carl smiled good-naturedly. "Jamey,

when you were in the car, did you find the lady's purse? Or anything else with any identification?"

"No. And there's nothing in the glove compartment either. The shoes were all there was."

Tom stared at his son, exasperated with himself that he'd been so distracted he'd taken his eyes off the boy at the scene of an accident.

"I think we'd better get this young lady to the hospital," Carl said.

Tom helped the other two men load the stretcher into the ambulance. His heart went out to the woman, whose face reflected her struggle against panic for some kind of control. Would her memory come back? What happened to people whose memory never returned? Surely she had a family to care for her, relatives who were looking for her even now. A husband maybe. But what if she didn't?

As the ambulance pulled onto the highway, Tom stared mutely after it. He and the boy should go back home now. There were a hundred chores that needed doing. But the image of those confused, determined, lovely eyes had grabbed him by the throat and wouldn't let go.

"Are we going to the hospital, Dad?" Jamey asked hopefully. "To see if she's all right?"

Tom looked down at his son's anxious expression. *Oh, hell,* he thought, *what's a couple of hours in the grand scheme of things anyway?* He ruffled Jamey's hair. "I'll tell you what, partner. Let's go feed the animals. Then we'll get cleaned up and go to the hospital to see how the lady's doing."

"Thanks, Dad!"

He and his son turned and headed back to the pickup truck. The little boy leapt over a mud puddle, barely clearing it with his well-worn sneakers.

Jamey let out a whoop and pointed to the sky. "Look, Dad! A rainbow!"

Two

She removed the cold compress from her forehead and gingerly ran her fingers over the bruise. An impressive lump had formed there, but that was the least of her problems. After a battery of tests, the doctors had informed her that she was not seriously injured, and that her memory could return anytime. So why hadn't it? They were about to release her, and she had no idea where to go. What in the world was she going to do?

As she picked up the plastic bag of toiletries the hospital had given her, a short, humorless laugh escaped her. If she was going to be a homeless bag lady, it was nice of them to give her a bag at least, a sort of head start in life. She rummaged through the bag—toothbrush, toothpaste, lotion, comb, mirror. *Mirror.*

Since she'd regained consciousness, she'd been concentrating with all her might, trying to remember who she was. She grabbed the mirror and stared hard at herself. A pale, frightened stranger stared back. She stifled a bout of hysterical laughter. She'd really expected to recognize herself, to look in the mirror and be able to say, "Oh, it's *you.*" No such luck.

She threw the mirror back into the bag in disgust and collapsed onto the pillows. "Ow!" The sudden movement brought back her killer headache and a fresh wave of dizziness. As she lay there, she felt icy fingers of panic creep up her spine. *Relax,* she commanded herself. But that was easier said than done when you didn't know if you were going to have a roof over your head tonight.

Tom and Jamey started down the sterile green corridor, Tom's boots making too much noise on the shiny linoleum floor. He hated hospitals.

They reached a nurses' station where the maze of corridors intersected. Tom saw Sheriff Harvey Gulch leaning on the tall counter, flirting with one of the nurses. "We'll ask the nurse how she is," he told Jamey. "We don't want to disturb the lady who was in the accident." He stepped up to the counter, waiting his turn to speak to the woman in white, and exchanged nods with the sheriff.

"Dorothy!" Jamey exclaimed, and disappeared through a doorway of one of the patient rooms.

"Jamey, wait!" Tom hurried after his son.

In the sterile white room, she was thumbing through the phone book trying to jog her memory for names when the little boy burst in. "Dorothy," he'd said. He knew her—her name was Dorothy! The name *did* have a ring of familiarity about it. Maybe her memory was coming back! She studied the child to see if she could recognize him. He was stocky, a bit rumpled, but clean. His overalls, T-shirt, and sneakers were so worn, they were probably hand-me-downs. No one kid could put that many miles on clothes and shoes, surely. A shock of shaggy black hair fell over one eye, and a smattering of freckles covered his rosy cheeks.

He must know her, she thought, because the smile that lit up that angel's face said he was delighted to see her. Was this her child? Then she remembered that he had called her Dorothy, not Mom. She felt a pang of disappointment.

As she tried to place the child in her memory, a form appeared behind him. She raised her eyes to see a very big, very attractive man. Surely she couldn't have forgotten a man like this, she told herself, but a hopeful warmth spread through her just the same. Actually, he *did* look familiar. Was this *her* man? If so, it must have been one hell of an accident, because she'd evidently just died and gone to heaven.

Six foot three if he was an inch, the man dominated the room. But even more impressive than his powerful, muscular build was his face. Its rough-hewn beauty took her breath away as he removed his baseball cap and ran a hand through a crop of thick, black hair. The hue of his gray-green eyes was accentuated by dark brows and lashes and a tan so deep it could only have come from working long hours outdoors.

He replaced his cap, then touched its bill in an old-fashioned gesture of respect. "Please excuse my son, ma'am. He gets a little carried away sometimes."

He didn't know her. She felt disappointment again, stronger this time. Now she remembered. This man and his little boy had been at the crash site when they loaded her into the ambulance. She supposed she should be grateful she remembered that much at least.

"Are you going to be okay?" the little boy asked, his expression solemn.

The man stepped forward and laid a restraining hand on the child's shoulder. "I'm Tom Weaver and this is my son, Jamey. We were the ones who found you and called for help. We just thought we'd come by and see how you are. But we don't want to disturb you. If you're not feeling well, we'll go."

"No. Don't go." The stranger's concern touched her deeply. "It's very kind of you to come to see me. The doctors tell me that I'm going to be all right. But I still don't know who I am."

"*I* know who you are," the boy said, grinning a gap-toothed grin. "You're Dorothy."

"Jamey, don't start that again," Tom said in gentle admonishment. Then to her, "My son is a big fan of *The Wizard of Oz*. He's probably seen it a hundred times—you know how kids are. When he saw you unconscious after the tornado, well . . ."

She had to laugh despite herself. "I guess the similarities are pretty obvious."

Tom relaxed when he heard her laugh, the musical sound touching him someplace deep inside that he'd forgotten even existed.

Jamey piped up again. "When are they going to let you out of here?"

"Anytime now."

She looked small and vulnerable in the hospital gown, although she was putting on a brave face. "Where do you go from here?" Tom asked.

"I don't know." Her nervous smile disappeared altogether. "The sheriff says the town doesn't have any women's shelters, but he said I can spend the night in jail."

Something in Tom's heart twisted. Before he could stop the boy, Jamey scrambled up on the foot of her hospital bed. "You can't go to jail! You didn't do anything wrong. You can stay with us. Can't she, Dad?"

Tom looked from Jamey, his expression imploring, to the woman sitting at the far end of the bed. She pulled the sheet higher in a protective gesture, as if weighing the alternatives of a night in jail versus going home with strangers.

She lifted her chin and said, "I couldn't impose on you like that. You don't even know me."

"Yes we do. You're Dorothy. And we're going to help you. Please come home with us."

The woman did not protest again. She only looked at Tom with luminous eyes. The eyes were brave and did not plead. It was her strength that won him over, more effectively than any plea for pity could have. He heard himself say, "Yes, please stay with us. You'd be welcome."

The woman smiled, looking from him to Jamey and back again. "Are you sure it wouldn't be too much trouble?"

"Of course not," Tom said.

"Yay," cried Jamey, clapping his hands. "Dorothy's coming with us!"

"Jamey," Tom began, "maybe the lady has another name she'd like to be called."

The woman shrugged. "Until my memory comes back, and if it makes Jamey happy, Dorothy it is."

A nurse appeared in the doorway. "I have your discharge papers," she told Dorothy. "I'll help you get dressed."

Tom lifted Jamey off the bed. "We'll be right outside." His heart quickened at her smile of gratitude, and he walked back into the hallway and set his son down. He released a pent-up breath and leaned against the wall as Jamey wandered over to inspect a child-sized water fountain. The sheriff had apparently finished flirting with the nurse and walked down the hall toward them.

"Hello, Tom. Carl said you and Jamey were the ones who found the mystery woman in the wrecked Caddy." The sheriff jerked his thumb toward the closed door to Dorothy's room.

Mystery woman. Tom rolled his eyes to the ceiling. You'd think she was a spy, for crying out loud. He knew Sheriff Harvey Gulch to be a bit on the dramatic side. Because there was so little crime in the small town and surrounding county, he tended to blow any suspicious activity out of proportion. Especially when he was up for reelection, which he was now. With an overdeveloped upper body supported by spindly legs, he looked and acted like Barney Fife on steroids.

"That's right. We just came to see how she was, and since she doesn't seem to have anywhere else to go, we thought we'd let her stay with us tonight."

The lawman's expression became grave. "I don't know if I'd advise that, Tom." He cut his eyes at Jamey, who was still occupied with the fountain, and lowered his voice. "I have reason to believe our Jane Doe might be a perp."

"A perp?"

"You know, a perpetrator." Harvey looked at him as if he were the village idiot.

"Just because she doesn't know who she is?"

Harvey took his hat off and scratched the stubble on his head. "It's not just that. I stopped to take a look at that car on the way over here. There's no tag, and the vehicle identification number has been filed off."

That was unusual, Tom allowed. "So you think the car is stolen?"

"Of course. And that amnesia story—give me a break." He gave a derisive snort of laughter.

Tom glanced at Jamey uneasily. "What do you mean?"

"It sure is a convenient way not to have to answer any questions about yourself and why you're in a stolen car." The sheriff put his hat back on and adjusted it to its usual cocky angle with both hands. "Don't you worry, though. I'll know who she is before long."

Jamey walked back over to them and Harvey patted him awkwardly on the head. "Just remember," the sheriff said as he started to walk away, "if it looks like a duck and walks like a duck . . ."

Harvey let his last statement trail off for dramatic effect. When he was out of earshot, Jamey observed, *"He* walks like a duck and he ain't a duck."

Tom smiled and ruffled his son's hair. Jamey was right. He hadn't heard enough to convince him that the woman was a criminal. She certainly didn't look dangerous. Besides, he was a man of his word, and if he said she could stay the night with him and Jamey, then—

Dorothy stepped into the hallway beside them, causing Tom to lose his train of thought. She was again wearing the black dress and red jacket, along with the red pumps. He might have been a little hasty when he'd thought she didn't look dangerous. His eyes took her in, from the toes of her snakeskin shoes to her head full of golden-brown hair.

She looked plenty dangerous.

On the pickup truck ride to the farm, Dorothy looked in vain for any kind of landmark that would cause her to remember something—anything. But there was only farmland, with a nondescript house here and there. Nothing looked familiar. Not even the crumpled Cadillac still on the side of the road. She shuddered when she saw its mangled frame. For the first time that day, she felt lucky. Looking at the wreckage, she realized it was a miracle she wasn't injured more seriously than she had been. She closed her eyes for a moment and uttered a silent prayer of thanks.

The little boy kept up a constant chatter on the way. He couldn't wait to introduce her to his dog, his horse, his favorite pig. The man was quiet. Dorothy sneaked a sidelong glance at him from time to time. He had a beautifully chiseled profile—high cheekbones, full lips, perfect nose and strong chin. His mouth curled into a lazy grin whenever his son said something that amused him.

Jamey's mother was a lucky woman. Dorothy wondered if Tom had called home to warn his wife that he was bringing home a houseguest, a stranger. The thought made her uneasy. Maybe she wouldn't be welcome. "Will your wife mind letting me stay the night at your house?" She noticed the animation drain from Jamey's face as he looked down at his sneakers.

Tom's jaw became set in a hard line. "My wife divorced me about a year ago."

"I'm sorry," she said quickly.

She was trying to think of something to say to fill the awkward silence when Tom turned off the road onto a long dirt driveway flanked by fields of corn. After a minute or two they came to a white frame farmhouse with a barn and several more outbuildings clustered around it. The house was small but neat and looked freshly painted. A porch went all the way around the house, and sported a swing and a couple of rockers in front. Tom drove to the back door.

Jamey sprang from the truck. "Toto! Come 'ere, boy. Dorothy's here to meet you. Toto!"

Dorothy alighted from the truck with a smile—the dog would be named Toto, of course. She walked toward the house. What she had at first taken for a wadded-up burlap bag on the porch began to move. "Toto?"

The ancient hound raised his listless head and thumped his tail on the porch floor. Loose folds of skin drooped around the dog's jowls and bloodshot eyes. The animal could not have looked less like its movie namesake. Jamey ran to him and gave him a fierce hug. Dorothy had to stifle a giggle. "Nice to meet you, Toto."

"His name used to be Blue." Tom passed by her,

handing her the plastic bag as he did. "You forgot your luggage." He winked.

"Thanks." She had to laugh even though the bag reminded her of the fact that she had only the clothes on her back, and not very practical ones at that. Tom seemed in a good mood once more, the mention of his ex-wife evidently forgotten.

Jamey remained on the porch playing with Toto as Tom went up the steps. She followed him through the door and into the kitchen. He stopped to hang his cap on a peg on the wall.

The kitchen was neat and spacious. The cabinets were painted a light yellow color, giving the room a sunny look, even in the early evening. A sturdy oak table with four matching chairs sat in the center of the room. Dorothy walked to it and ran her hand across the glass-like finish, admiring the workmanship and the quality and thickness of the wood. "This is a very nice table. They don't make them like this anymore."

He leaned against the wall, his large frame looking as solid as the oak on which Dorothy rested her hand. "Most people don't, but I do. I made it myself."

Genuinely impressed, Dorothy said, "Your work is excellent."

"Thanks. A lot of people don't recognize quality when they see it." He looked at her in a thoughtful, slightly critical way. "Maybe that's a clue to your identity. Maybe you're used to having fine things around you."

She shrugged, puzzled by his odd negative tone. "Maybe. Or maybe I was a furniture saleswoman."

They both laughed, and the brief moment of tension disappeared as quickly as it had come.

"Come on," he said. "I'll show you to your room, and then I'll see if I can find some clean clothes for you."

She followed him through a dining room to a foyer leading to the front door and the staircase to the second floor. The staircase was another piece of woodworking art. A well-built house for a well-built man, she thought. As she climbed the stairs behind him, she marveled at his massive shoulders and powerful back tapering to a trim waist and a truly remarkable derriere.

"This is Jamey's room," he said, pointing to the first bedroom they came to. Dorothy glanced into it as they passed. The neatly made bed was covered in a spread made out of print material with race cars all over it. A desk, chair, and toy chest lined the wall opposite the bed.

"And that's mine," he continued, indicating a closed door. He led her to a room at the end of the hallway and opened the door. "This was my sister's room before she got married," he said as she stepped inside.

The room charmed her immediately. The walls were covered with floral-patterned wallpaper in soft shades of pink, blue, and yellow. The bedspread was a quilt appliqued with matching flowers. A canopy, edged in what looked like hand-crocheted lace, gave the four-poster bed a feminine touch. The dresser was of the antique vanity variety, with a round mirror in the center and drawers on either side.

"It's lovely," Dorothy said simply as she stepped forward and touched the lace on the canopy.

"Bathroom's across the hall," Tom said from behind her. "There should be a new toothbrush in the medicine chest. I'll go get you some clothes."

She turned in a circle, taking in the whole room at once, then approached the vanity. It was another lovely piece. She ran her hand along the beveled edge of the mirror and felt a piece of cellophane tape. Looking at it more closely, she could see that a tiny, yellowed piece of paper was trapped beneath the tape. She smiled to herself. She thought she'd seen dressers like this in old television shows. Girls used to tape their mementos all along the outside edge of the mirror—banners from their high school, corsages from their boyfriends, that sort of thing.

What had that old scrap of paper been a part of? The girl's high school graduation invitation? A newspaper clipping? A letter of acceptance from her favorite university? Dorothy sighed. What had her own room looked like when she was growing up? She didn't even know what her favorite color was. Had she been a scholar? An athlete? A cheerleader? Would memories like this be lost to her forever?

Dorothy looked at her reflection again, more carefully than she had with the tiny mirror earlier. She looked no more familiar to herself than she had before. She wondered from whom she'd inherited her oval face, her unruly hair. Was it from her mother or her father? And were her mother and father looking for her now?

As she looked at the forlorn, bedraggled woman in the mirror, she noticed Tom's reflection over her shoulder.

Her eyes must have betrayed her mood, because he

stood motionless, as if caught between the desire to stay and comfort her, or retreat and leave her to her private thoughts. His eyes held only compassion.

"Sorry," she said, turning to face him and trying to manage a smile. "I guess I was feeling a little sorry for myself there for a minute."

"Don't apologize. I don't see how you've stayed as calm as you are. I don't know how I'd react if I'd been through the kind of trauma you've suffered today."

She had a powerful urge to be held by this man. He was so big and strong-looking, she felt as if she would be able to draw strength just from his touch. She might have run into his outstretched arms if not for the fact that they were already full of a neat stack of clothing.

"I've found you some clothes and shoes," he said, putting them on the bed. "You're a little taller than Margaret so the jeans may be a little short, but other than that I think they should fit you." His gaze traveled the length of her body in an appraising way. "Well, I'll leave you alone for a while. There are towels and washcloths in the hall closet if you want to take a shower or bath. Make yourself at home."

He hesitated for a moment, another look of indecision on his face. Then he reached out, cupped her chin lightly and said, "Chin up. Everything's going to be all right."

His skin was warm and rough but the touch had a tenderness that sent a tingling thrill up her spine. For the first time in her brief memory, Dorothy really believed everything might be all right, because he said so.

* * *

She slid into the sleek designer jeans, feeling like a new woman after her hot bath. For all intents and purposes she *was* a new woman, she thought wryly. It was as if she'd just been born, full-grown, like Athena, goddess of wisdom. *Yeah, right,* she thought. She was so wise she could remember obscure bits of mythology, but not her own name.

The short-sleeved cotton pullover felt wonderfully soft against her skin. It did feel a little weird wearing someone else's clothing, but beggars couldn't be choosers, and that's exactly what she was. The bag lady image came into her mind again, but she pushed it aside. Like Scarlett O'Hara, she would think about that tomorrow. Maybe her memory would be back by then. Maybe during a good night's sleep, her mind would somehow repair itself and she would wake up knowing who she was and where she belonged.

She found Tom in the kitchen removing a package of ground beef from the refrigerator. He turned to look at her and stood stock still for a moment, an odd look on his face.

"You were right. They fit fine," Dorothy said. "Be sure and tell your sister I said thanks for lending me some of her clothes."

Tom's expression became neutral, unreadable. "They're not my sister's clothes. They're my wife's." He turned away, facing the sink.

A shiver ran up her spine. She was wearing his ex-wife's clothes. No wonder he'd looked at her so oddly. She decided to change the subject before Tom turned to face her again. "Where's Jamey?"

"Finishing up his chores. He'll be in before dark and

just in time to eat supper." Tom rolled up his sleeves, revealing muscular, bronzed forearms covered with crisp black hair. He washed his hands carefully and began to pat out the hamburgers. "How's the head?"

"Oh, much better. When I was taking a bath I put a cool washcloth on it. The worst of the dizziness seems to be gone too."

"You know, I've heard some people use raw meat to treat bumps like that. How about it?" He took a handful of hamburger and made as if to place it against her forehead. Dorothy jumped aside just as he drew his hand away, laughing. "Only kidding."

"No thanks. My head looks bad enough without a hamburger sticking to it." She laughed, grateful that he had gone out of his way to lighten the mood. His little joke had seemed to put them both at ease.

"Your head looks okay to me." Tom's smile crinkled the corners of his remarkable green eyes and made him look like a teenager.

"Thanks, I appreciate that." She saw that he had placed some vegetables and a cutting board on the counter next to the sink. "Can I help you with anything?"

"Sure." He opened a drawer, removed a large chef's knife, and handed it to her, handle first. "Why don't you chop up some vegetables for a salad? There's a colander in the cabinet right in front of you. But before you can get it into the sink, you may have to put those dirty dishes in the dishwasher. That is, if you don't mind."

"Not at all." Dorothy managed to get the dishwasher open with some difficulty and slid out the bottom shelf.

Funny, this activity didn't seem familiar to her, she thought as she tentatively arranged the dishes in what she hoped was an acceptable manner. Out of the corner of her eye, she saw Tom watching her.

"It might be a good idea to put Jamey's plastic cups in the top rack. That way, they're less likely to fly around the dishwasher and then melt." He smiled tolerantly at her while arranging the hamburgers on a small electric grill next to the stove.

"Maybe I forgot how to use a dishwasher along with my memory," she offered sheepishly, rearranging the cups.

"Or maybe you never knew how to begin with."

Dorothy drew herself up as she put the colander in the sink. "Well, I suppose that's possible. Maybe I was too poor to be able to afford a dishwasher."

"Or too rich to have to use one." He leaned one hip on the cabinet and regarded her evenly, his dark brows drawing together slightly.

"That would be a nice alternative."

"If you say so."

She put her hands on her hips and looked at him with a mixture of amusement and consternation. "Didn't someone once say that they'd been rich, and they'd been poor, and rich was better?"

"I wouldn't know. I've only been poor, and I've known people who were rich and weren't as happy as me."

"Geez, I'll bet *they* were a barrel of laughs," Dorothy muttered under her breath as he crossed the kitchen to a dish cabinet. She picked up the chef's knife, wondering why he was copping an attitude.

"So, we've established that I'm either rich or I'm poor, nothing in between," she said in a light tone. "How are we going to figure out which scenario is the correct one?"

As Tom set the table, he gave her a sly look. "I know a way." He sauntered over to her, slowly and deliberately.

She noted, not for the first time, that for a large man, he moved quite gracefully. His walk was almost feline in its fluidity. She backed up as he approached her, her back pressed against the sink.

"First of all," he said in his deep baritone, "put down the knife."

"I don't know if I should," she said, grinning in spite of herself. "What's involved in this test you have in mind?"

"Oh, nothing dangerous. I will have to touch you, though."

"Oh?"

He took the knife from her and laid it on the counter. As his eyes held hers, he put his hands lightly on her shoulders, then let them slide slowly down her arms, igniting her senses as they went. His hands were rough, the skin of a working man, but his touch was gentle. The electrical sparks that touch struck along its path made her shiver and go warm all over at the same time.

When her hands were in his, he brought them together and opened his palms. Only then did he take his eyes from hers and begin a careful inspection of the hands he held. He turned them over, running his thumbs across her palms.

She inhaled sharply as a fresh wave of sensation

swept over her and settled somewhere in the pit of her stomach. "Are you going to read my palm?"

"In a way." He turned her hands over again and put both of them in one of his, running the other over the skin on the backs of her hands.

"You're a man of many talents, I see. If you have a crystal ball, maybe you can look into it and tell me what my name is." Her attempt at humor did nothing to dissipate the charge of sexual tension she felt from the mere touch of his hand, she realized.

"Sorry, no crystal ball," he said. "Your hands are nice and soft." He drew his calloused index finger across her knuckles. "You have a good manicure, too. Probably an expensive one, by the looks of it."

"So what does my palm tell you?" she asked, trying to keep her tone light. "You look pretty serious. Do I have a short lifeline or something?"

"It's not that," Tom said tersely. A frown crossed his face briefly like a passing storm cloud. Finally, after what seemed like hours, he took his gaze from her hands and let it travel lazily back to her face. One corner of his mouth crooked upward in a lopsided grin but no humor reached his glittering green eyes.

"What then?"

"It's just what I thought. You're a rich girl, all right. You've never done a lick of hard work in your life."

Three

Dorothy's mouth flew open in indignation. She jerked her hands away, feeling the shocking suddenness of the broken connection. "That's a terrible thing to say about a person," she said, rubbing her hands together to stop their tingling.

Tom crossed his arms and regarded her smugly. "You've never had a callus in your life."

She gripped the counter on either side of her. "Wait a minute. Just because I don't have calluses like yours doesn't mean I haven't done any work. Maybe I'm a scientist or mathematician or something."

"A scientist who doesn't know how to work a dishwasher?"

She glared at him. "I'll bet plenty of scientists don't know how to use dishwashers. Albert Einstein was brilliant, and they say he had no common sense whatsoever."

Tom smiled broadly, revealing even, white teeth. "Sounds like a great role model."

"You are the most exasperating man I've ever met!" Dorothy wheeled around to face the sink and grabbed the knife. She began to chop the lettuce furiously, sending bits of the green stuff flying.

Tom sauntered closer until he stood an arm's length from her, his insolent gaze causing a pull in her stomach. "That's not much of a distinction since I'm probably the *only* exasperating man you can remember meeting. Still, something tells me you wish that was *my* head on that chopping block instead of a head of lettuce."

"Do you have any idea how frustrating this is?" She turned and gestured toward him with the knife, causing him to take a step backward and raise his hands in a mock defensive posture. "I can recall obscure facts about Albert Einstein, but I can't even remember my own name." She raked the chopped lettuce into the colander.

"I know this is a difficult time for you. I'm sorry for giving you a hard time." Tom gave her a contrite look and turned on the water to wash the lettuce. "There is something else, though."

"What?" She tried to peel one of the carrots, but it was difficult with the huge knife.

"Well, for one thing, you're peeling off so much of the carrot, there's not going to be any left. You just need to scrape them off some. Here, let me." He took the knife from her.

She moved aside to let him stand in front of the cutting board. "Great. So my insufficient vegetable chopping skills reinforces your theory that I'm a spoiled brat who doesn't know her way around the kitchen."

"No, that's not what I was going to say." Tom paused, as if trying to decide whether to go on. "When I looked

at your hands, I noticed something else besides your
soft skin and lack of calluses. I think you're a married
lady."

"How do you know that?" she demanded.

Tom did not raise his eyes from his work as he spoke.
"Look very carefully at the ring finger on your left
hand and tell me what you see."

She saw what he meant immediately. Why hadn't she
noticed it herself? There was a pale band of flesh running across her finger, that and a slight indentation. A
ring had been there. Had been there for a long time.
And it hadn't been long since it had been removed.
What had happened to it?

"I see what you mean," she said slowly, rubbing the
mark with the fingers of her right hand. "We can't know
for sure it was a wedding ring, though. It could have
been a class ring, or any kind of ring, for that matter."

He looked sidelong at her. "On the left hand?"

He had a point. Most women reserved their left ring
finger for engagement and wedding rings. The idea of
being married seemed strange somehow. She didn't feel
married. Or was it that she didn't want to be married?
She looked at the man beside her and saw that he was
frowning again. Was he simply concentrating on his
work or was there something about this conversation
that disturbed him too?

"Listen," Tom began in a voice as soft and deep as
velvet. "I'm really sorry for giving you a hard time."
He hesitated, and she sensed that he was trying to decide whether to say more. "It's just that I have this
friend, another farmer, and he married a rich city girl.

She was never happy on the farm, and he wasn't happy because she wasn't happy."

She picked up a carrot from the cutting board and munched it thoughtfully. "Sounds pretty miserable."

"Yeah, it was."

She watched him turn the vegetables from the colander into a large salad bowl. Surely there was more to his puzzling demeanor than the experience of his friend. He went from moody to friendly and back again with dizzying speed. It was as if there were two Toms— Farmer Jekyll and Mr. Hyde.

She had opened her mouth to ask him to tell her more about his friend when Jamey burst in.

"Dad, do I have time to show Dorothy the animals before supper?"

"Not tonight, partner. We've gotten a late start on supper and it's almost dark. There'll be plenty of time for that in the morning. Now, go get washed up."

Jamey looked at her, shrugged, and raced for the stairs. Dorothy looked after him, smiling. "Are all the animals as impressive as Toto?"

Tom looked at her in mock reproach. "I'll have you know most of them still have their own teeth."

Dorothy hadn't realized how hungry she was until she started the meal, and she wound up eating a generous portion of everything. She couldn't hold a candle to the guys, though. Tom had the healthy appetite of a man who did plenty of physical work and Jamey ate like a typical growing boy. Between bites, Jamey told her how much he looked forward to going to school in the fall.

Tom interjected comments here and there but let his son do most of the talking.

As they cleared the table, the boy asked, "Can Dorothy and I watch TV?"

"Okay, but only for thirty minutes or so, then it's bedtime. You two run along. I'll finish up in here."

Dorothy let the boy lead her by the hand into a den just off the dining room. She hadn't noticed the den when she'd gone through the house before. It was a comfortably masculine room with dark, rough paneling and traditional furniture. Floor-to-ceiling bookshelves lined two walls, and a bank of windows made up another. The fourth was covered with framed photographs. An open rolltop desk in one corner was strewn with papers.

Jamey positioned himself on the cushy sofa and Dorothy sat beside him. He used the remote to turn on the television to a children's program. They discussed Jamey's favorite shows and cartoons as they watched television, and after a while, the boy became so interested in the program that he seemed to forget Dorothy was there. She got up to stretch her legs and look around the room.

The shelves held a huge variety of books. One whole section was devoted to agriculture and animal husbandry. Just the sort of books you would expect to find on a modern farm. There were more nonfiction books on a multiplicity of subjects as well as a set of encyclopedias and accompanying children's volumes. There were novels too, particularly detective whodunits and westerns.

After strolling past the shelves, she reached the far

wall, which was devoted to an arrangement of family photos. There were several portraits and a group shot of Tom's family. She peered at the family photo, taken on the front porch right outside. She'd know the older man anywhere—Tom looked just like his father. His mother was a lovely woman with dark hair and fine features. Tom's sister looked like a younger version of her mother.

She stared at the photos wistfully. Did she herself have a sister? A brother? Had they had time to discover that she was missing? Perhaps they were looking for her, were worried about her.

She shook herself and returned her attention to the photo of Tom. The teenaged Tom was handsome in a youthful way, with all the promise of the devastatingly attractive man he was destined to grow into. She'd just bet every girl in the county had been after him.

There were other photos of Tom as well, including a graduation portrait and two pictures of him in a football uniform—one high school and the other college, she guessed. She couldn't help but notice that although there were two or three photos of Jamey, there were none of his mother. She supposed the divorce must have been very painful for Tom to have removed any family photos containing images of his ex-wife.

"Meet the family," the deep voice behind her said.

Startled, she jumped, causing him to laugh and lay a steadying hand on her shoulder. His touch, casual though it was, caused her body to come alive, just as it had in the kitchen earlier. She longed to lean back against his massive chest, to feel his torso against the curve of her back, but she resisted the urge.

"Steady, there. I didn't mean to scare you." He gave her shoulder a friendly pat and then removed his hand. "Motley crew, eh?"

"Not at all. You have a lovely family," she said, her fingers creeping involuntarily upward to feel the warmth his hand had left behind.

"Mom and Dad are out in Montana now. Mom's family was in ranching, and she inherited a big spread out there right before Jamey was born. She and Dad moved out there to manage it, but they come back pretty often to visit." He pointed at a portrait of his sister. "Casey married a farmer and lives on the other side of the county."

"I guess your parents were proud when you and your sister decided to follow their footsteps and stay in farming."

"I suppose so. I guess most parents are pleased whenever their kids decide to carry on the family business." Tom's full lips tugged upward in a lazy grin, and he leaned one shoulder against the wall and just looked at her.

His gaze drifted from her hair to her mouth, and briefly, to her breasts. She flinched, almost as if she could feel his touch everywhere his gaze wandered. It seemed that his every word and breath and look was an exercise in sensuality. If she looked at him long enough, she felt almost feverish. Why would any woman give up a man like this?

His emerald gaze finally returned to her eyes, and he straightened. "If you'll excuse me, I have some paperwork to do." He indicated the ledgers and stacks of paper on the rolltop desk and sighed. "It's not exactly my favorite part of farming, and I tend to let it pile up. But we can't afford a bookkeeper, so that's another of the many hats I wear, along with chief cook and bottle washer."

"I'd volunteer to help you with the bookkeeping, but I'm afraid I wouldn't know which end of a ledger was up. I can't even remember if I know how to balance a checkbook or run a computer."

Tom laughed and patted her shoulder again. "I appreciate the offer. But since I have my own special system of bookkeeping, accounting, and filing, you probably wouldn't be able to pick up where I've left off even if you were a certified public accountant."

Dorothy walked back to the sofa and sat beside Jamey as Tom took up his place at the desk. She was beginning to realize how much responsibility Tom had on his shoulders. The work involved with running a farm did not end when the last of the animals was fed at night. It sounded like a twenty-four-hour job. It made her wish there was something she could do to help him. Surely she had some kind of skills. If she could just remember what she had done for a living before that damned tornado had given her the head injury.

At eight-thirty, Tom called from across the big room, "Bedtime, partner."

Jamey reluctantly turned off the TV and wriggled his way off the couch. "G'night," he said. As he reached the doorway, he hesitated, and then turned around and headed back to the couch. Standing beside her, he raised his arms in a clear invitation for a hug.

Dorothy was touched by the little boy's affection. She leaned forward and wrapped her arms around him. "Good night, sweetie," she whispered. She had the impression that five-year-old boys had usually reached a stage where they didn't want hugs and kisses from people they didn't know well, and sometimes not even from people they did. But Jamey welcomed affection from her, probably because he missed his mother so much. She sat back and wondered why she knew all this with so much conviction. While talking to Jamey, she'd made a real connection with him. It felt very normal and natural communicating with the boy. Maybe she had been a kindergarten teacher or something.

After a moment, she patted his back gently and let him go. He smiled and left the room, a spring now in his little-boy swagger.

She sighed and then a warmth spread through her. She felt the heat of Tom's stare as surely as she'd felt the intimate connection of his earlier touch. Slowly, she raised her gaze to meet his. His eyes, green and catlike beneath their heavy brows and thick fringe of black lashes, regarded her with a searching wariness.

The intensity of his expression made her involuntarily cross her arms in a protective gesture. The look on Tom's face coupled with her musings about Jamey made her realize something. She had noted from the beginning how nice Tom had been to her, but she now was particularly struck by the magnitude of his kindness. Taking her, a stranger, into his home meant trusting her with the one possession in his life he obviously prized above all others—his son.

"I think I'll turn in too," she blurted, rising to her feet.

"Have a good night's rest," he said evenly. "You've had a hell of a day."

She smiled weakly and started for the door. At the

threshold, she turned back, watching his thoughtful profile as he returned his attention to his work. This man had opened his home to her, a stranger, had given her food, clothing, and shelter. And he had trusted her to be around his son. He was a generous man. "Thank you again," she said, "for taking care of me."

He looked up at her and smiled. "You're welcome." His eyes had lost their wariness, and held only compassion. "Don't worry. We'll find your home, Dorothy. And you won't even have to follow a yellow brick road."

Something in her grateful smile pinched his heart. Tom watched her as she turned and walked from the room, admiring how her hourglass figure filled out the snug jeans, and how her glorious hair cascaded down her slender back. She was so damned beautiful, it almost hurt to look at her. He hadn't felt a hormone rush like this since he was in high school—hell, in his whole life. He'd barely been able to keep his hands off of her. He must have put his hand on her arm or shoulder at least three times.

How typical of his luck with women that fate had to send him an irresistible, gorgeous, rich city girl who was already taken. He tossed his pencil onto the desk and propped his head in his hand.

Thanks for taking care of me, she'd said. Too bad that taking care of females was something that he was absolutely abysmal at. Because against his better judgment, he'd like nothing more than to take care of this one.

* * *

The little ceramic lamp cast a warm glow onto the bedroom, giving it a cozy, inviting feel for which Dorothy was grateful. From the stack of clothing Tom had given her, she removed a white nightgown trimmed in eyelet lace and yellow ribbon. She put the garment to her cheek and felt its soft, smooth, combed cotton finish. Had this been a gift from Tom to his wife? It was an expensive-looking gown, of a much finer quality than the clothes Tom and Jamey wore. Perhaps he'd splurged for a special occasion. Had she actually worn it on the night he'd given it to her, or had it wound up on the floor?

She cursed herself for letting her mind stray to where it shouldn't and slipped out of her clothes and into the nightgown. Still, she couldn't help but run her palms across the material, imagining what Tom's touch would feel like through the fine fabric. Or better yet, without the fabric between them at all. She sighed, slipped into bed, and turned off the light.

She hadn't realized how tired she was until she crawled under the covers and closed her eyes. Maybe tomorrow she would have an identity, a past, a place to belong. Or maybe, she thought with a prickly pang of fear, she'd still have a cloud of mystery hanging over her head, obscuring her old life, whatever it had been.

Her doubts and fears finally dissolved into a fitful sleep in which she dreamt of a tiger with emerald green eyes.

Dorothy awoke the next morning, squinting against the sunlight streaming through the windows of her bedroom, and wondered where the hell she was. It took her a couple of minutes to become oriented to her surroundings. When it came back to her where she was and why she was here, she closed her eyes again and tried with all her might to remember who she was. Her mind struggled to come up with faces, places, names, anything. Nothing came.

She climbed out of bed slowly, her muscles still stiff and aching from yesterday's ordeal. As she donned the terry robe Tom had given her yesterday, she looked at herself in the vanity mirror. The bruise on her head looked much better, but her face was still that of a stranger. She slid her feet into shoes and started downstairs. By the look of the sunlight, she must have slept until midmorning.

As she crossed the threshold from the dining room to the kitchen, she heard heavy clomping steps ascending the porch. Then came Tom's voice. "Howdy, Sheriff."

Dorothy froze and pulled the robe more tightly around her. She remembered being questioned by the sheriff the day before. The man had not been friendly and sympathetic like the others at the hospital. In fact, his attitude had been accusing, as if he thought she'd done something wrong. He had given her a major case of the creeps, and she didn't particularly want to talk to him again, especially since she wasn't dressed.

Still, she wanted to hear what he had to say in case he had found out something about who she was and where she belonged. She paused beside the refrigerator and tried to figure out what to do. She could see the two men through the partially open porch door, but she didn't think they could see her. She felt a pang of guilt for eavesdropping on one of Tom's conversations, but she didn't know what else to do. She felt as if she were rooted to the spot where she was standing.

"Morning, Tom," the sheriff said, removing his dark aviator sunglasses with a flourish.

"So did you find out anything?" Tom's tone seemed nonchalant, but there was tension in his stance.

The sheriff removed his hat. Dorothy could see through his closely-cropped hair the crease the hat had made in his fleshy scalp. She shivered in disgust.

After a dramatic pause, the sheriff intoned, "I think so."

"Does she match any missing persons reports?" Tom asked anxiously.

"No." The sheriff continued to look smug.

"Does she have any warrants out against her?"

Warrants? Did they think she was a criminal? Dorothy leaned forward to get a better look at Tom's profile. His expression was stern with his eyes narrowed on the sheriff. His jaw was set so hard a muscle in his cheek twitched slightly.

"Well, no," the lawman admitted.

"Then what?"

"It's only a theory at this point. But if it pans out, it would explain a lot about what's been going on in this county the last few months."

"What are you talking about?" Tom asked in exasperation.

Crouched behind the refrigerator, Dorothy held her breath. She didn't like the sound of this. Not one bit. Then she saw the predatory gleam in the sheriff's eyes.

"A crime ring. And unless I miss my guess, our mystery woman is at the center of it."

Dorothy gasped, almost losing her balance, leaning as she was. She righted herself and pressed her back against the side of the refrigerator. They *did* think she was a criminal! Surely Tom wouldn't let her stay here another night if he thought she was a crook. Not that she expected to have to stay long. Surely her memory would come back any minute, but she'd rather not live in a jail cell until it did.

"What are you basing that theory on, Harvey?" Tom said evenly.

"We've had a string of burglaries in this part of the county and a couple of armed holdups as well. I think it's outsiders, and she could be part of it, especially turning up like she did, in that suspicious vehicle and claiming to have amnesia."

Dorothy peeked around the refrigerator again, to see Tom's arms crossed in a defensive gesture, slouched against the doorjamb, his chin thrust out, looking as stubborn as a mule. This was a good sign, she thought. He wasn't buying into the sheriff's theory.

Untroubled by Tom's sullen silence, Sheriff Gulch continued, "The tornado did some damage to several homes, so the relief agencies have their hands full. Ordinarily, I'd ask one of the church women in the community if they'd take her on as a boarder. But my suspicions being what they are, I couldn't recommend it. I strongly advise you to let me take her to jail until we find out something definite." The sheriff clasped his broad hands together and popped his knuckles.

"She'll stay here," Tom said simply.

The sheriff was incredulous. "Tom, you've got Jamey to think about."

Tom was in the sheriff's face before the other man could finish his sentence. "Nobody knows better than I do what's good for Jamey. I'm not going to let you take that woman to jail when all you have against her is a theory. You don't even have anything to charge her with."

The sheriff rocked so far back on the heels of his cowboy boots that Dorothy was sure his top-heavy body would topple over. He took a step back just in time, however, saving himself from a tumble down the porch steps and putting a more comfortable distance between himself and the very annoyed, very large farmer.

"Have it your way, but I'd be careful if I were you." Sheriff Gulch put his hat back on and replaced his sunglasses as if these items helped to restore some of his authority. "I want you to know I'm not going to rest until I find out who that girl is. I'll be in touch." With that, the man descended the steps and strutted to his car like a bantam rooster with a badge.

Dorothy heaved a sigh of relief as she heard the sheriff's car start. Tom was going to let her stay. But for how long? The next thing she heard was Tom's footsteps entering the kitchen and the slam of the porch door. Instinctively, she jumped back into the dining room. Then she heard chair legs scraping against the linoleum as Tom pulled out a chair from the table and sat down.

She made a spur-of-the-moment decision not to let Tom know she'd overheard him and the sheriff. Things would be less awkward that way. She took a moment to compose herself, took a deep breath, and strode into the kitchen as nonchalantly as she could manage. "Good morning. I'm sorry I slept so long." She yawned and stretched.

Tom's elbows were propped on the table, his head in his hands, obviously deep in thought. He looked up when she entered but did not smile. "Don't be. You went through a lot yesterday." He slowly looked her up and down. "I don't suppose your memory woke up when you did."

"No. I'm afraid not." Her hands went to the lapels of the robe, pulling it tighter again. She was once more aware that she was wearing his ex-wife's clothing. "Was that the sheriff I saw going down the driveway just now?"

"Yes." Tom stood up and walked to the counter. "Do you want some coffee?"

"Sure." She pulled a chair out from the table and sat down. He seemed so pensive. Was he reconsidering letting her stay here? "Does he know who I am?"

Tom returned with two mugs full of steaming coffee. "No, he doesn't." He set one of the mugs down in front of her and resumed his place at the table.

Dorothy took a sip of the coffee, studying Tom over the rim of the cup. His T-shirt was so soft and worn that she could see the definition of all the muscles in his chest. She had to force her attention away from his killer physique in order to concentrate on the matters at hand. "So did he say what happens now?"

"I'm sure the sheriff has some ideas. He said he wouldn't rest until he finds out who you are." Tom smiled pleasantly, obviously trying to reassure her. And she would have been reassured—if she hadn't overheard the sheriff and the malice with which he'd made that vow.

One of them had to broach the subject of where she was going to stay. She slipped one hand under the table and crossed her fingers. "I'm sure it won't be long. After all, I've been missing less than twenty-four hours. Maybe nobody has had a chance to miss me yet. Does the sheriff still want me to stay at the jail?"

Tom stared into his coffee cup as if it contained magic tea leaves he could read to see into the future. Finally, he looked up at her. "He did mention that, but I think I have a better idea."

"Oh?" She drew in a deep breath and crossed her fingers more tightly.

The barest hint of a smile crossed his face and disappeared into a mask of nonchalance. "I've got a proposition for you."

Four

Dorothy paused with her coffee cup halfway to her mouth, and eyed him with suspicion. "What kind of proposition?"

Tom chuckled at her reaction. It was a low, rumbling sound, thoroughly masculine and definitely disturbing.

"I'm in the middle of planting season and it's been rough because I don't have anyone to watch Jamey while I work. I've been taking him out to the fields with me, but even a five-year-old gets tired of riding a tractor after a while." Tom leaned back in his chair and smiled. Weariness had crept into his expression. "Anyway, since you'll be needing a place to stay for a while, I wondered if you'd be interested in taking care of Jamey and doing some light housework in exchange for room and board. I might be able to pay you a little but it wouldn't be much more than pocket money, I'm afraid. We've had some setbacks in the last year or so, and things are a little tight around here."

Dorothy looked at Tom with a renewed sense of respect. First he had put a positive spin on the sheriff's words in order to protect her feelings. And now he was offering her an opportunity to accept his food and shelter while preserving her dignity. His generosity made her speechless.

"It wouldn't be charity," he said gently, as if reading her thoughts in her silence. "I really do need your help. I realize that your memory will probably come back in a day or two. Either that or the sheriff will be able to identify you soon. But even if it's only a couple of days, you'd be doing me a favor if you decided to stay."

"Thank you. I accept." She thought about their conversation last night and about the workload that Tom had on his shoulders. She had wished then that she knew of a way that she could help him, to repay him. And now he had given her a way. She was thrilled.

Tom smiled broadly and extended his hand. She took it, and they shook on their agreement. Dorothy reveled in the warmth and strength of his grasp. Gazing at him, she felt the businesslike handshake change into something else—a caress. The roughness of his skin contrasted with the gentleness of his touch and sent a tingling sensation up her spine. Some elemental instinct told her that although he might be as big as a bear, this man was capable of great tenderness. This knowledge throbbed throughout all the feminine places in her body and soul.

His smile changed into an expression that spoke of the tenderness she sensed. And something else—longing, she thought. He inhaled sharply. The atmosphere in the kitchen seemed to change somehow, and all her senses became sharply focused. Tom's eyes took on a sea green intensity that drew her closer to him, and he leaned toward her, his full lips parting slightly. She was drawn to him as if by a powerful force.

Jamey burst through the door with a suddenness that startled both her and Tom, causing them to sit bolt upright. "My chores are done. Can I show Dorothy the animals now?"

Dorothy was shaken to realize that her face had been only inches from Tom's, and from his expression, so was he. Flustered, she ran a hand through her hair and gave Jamey a smile. "Sure, I'll just go and change." Dorothy took the excuse to leave the table and head for her room.

"Wait," Tom called after her.

Almost to the dining room door, she turned and looked shyly at him, still embarrassed, although by what she wasn't sure. She didn't know exactly what it was that had just passed between them before Jamey came in, but she felt her body still glowing from it.

Tom paused, as if deciding what to say. "Don't you want any breakfast? There's ham and eggs."

"No, thanks. The coffee was enough."

"You should keep up your strength, you know." His voice betrayed the almost imperceptible strain of forced casualness.

Dorothy smiled, touched anew by his concern. "I'm fine. Thanks. I'll be right back down after I shower and change."

He said no more but continued to gaze at her, motionless, expressionless. She found it difficult to turn from him again, but she did. Jamey may not have picked up on the emotionally charged atmosphere, but he would if she didn't leave, if she didn't break contact with Tom.

She turned around and headed for the stairs. As she passed the door to Tom's bedroom, she hesitated. The door, which had been closed every time she'd ever passed it, was open halfway. She could see his bed, neatly made, more or less, with a plain quilt for a spread. *His bed.* She gripped the door frame to support her suddenly shaky legs and cursed under her breath. What the hell was she doing going weak-kneed over a man she'd known for less than a day? Especially when there was a pretty good chance she might be married to someone else.

Dorothy took a deep breath and forced herself to continue down the hallway toward the bathroom. Better make that shower a cold one, she thought. She needed something to shock her back to her senses, and get her mind off the tall, dark, *very* handsome farmer. But something told her that it would take more than a cold shower.

Tom swore savagely as he drove the pitchfork into a mound of hay. He'd almost kissed her! What had he been thinking? She was probably married, for God's sake. He tossed the forkful of hay aside, startling several chickens who scattered in all directions, squawking indignantly.

For that matter, why had he even asked her to stay? The sheriff might have been right. No, he couldn't believe she was a crook. He stabbed the pitchfork into the ground and leaned heavily on the handle. Who was he kidding? He knew exactly why he had asked her to stay. Had it been so long since he'd been close to a pretty woman that he lost his wits over one? No, that wasn't it. Plenty of women had tried to get close to him in the year since Margaret had left. He just hadn't felt right about seeing someone so soon. Not that he felt right about it now. But there was something about Dorothy he couldn't resist.

He didn't know what had come over him in the kitchen just now, didn't know where that almost magnetic pull between them had come from, but he knew he couldn't let it happen again. To become involved with a woman only to have her taken from him, as she surely would be, was insanity. He'd keep their relationship on a businesslike level, and when her memory returned in a couple of days, that would be the end of it.

He sighed. Loneliness had been with him so long, it was part of him. Maybe his sister was right. Maybe it was time that he started looking for someone to share his life. But it couldn't be Dorothy, or whatever her name was. He'd bet his bottom dollar she was a rich city girl, and a married one at that. He just wished she didn't have eyes a man could get lost in.

Across the yard, he heard the screen door slam and looked up. Jamey was leading her toward him by the hand. She was laughing her musical laugh and the breeze was stirring her hair. He took a deep breath and swallowed hard. "Why me, Lord?" he muttered under his breath. "Why am I always attracted to the wrong woman?"

* * *

The midmorning sun shone brightly in a cloudless sky as Dorothy and Jamey crossed the barnyard. Dorothy took a deep breath of the clean country air and had the sense that she wasn't used to it. She appreciated it too much. Perhaps Tom was right. Maybe she was a city girl. She saw him staring at her as he leaned on a pitchfork, a semiscowl on his face. Was that for her or the world in general? she wondered. She waved weakly as Jamey led her toward a corral. Tom nodded and gave her a grudging half-grin.

When they reached the corral, Jamey jumped onto the bottom rail and grabbed the top one with both hands so that he could look over it. The corral contained a single horse, one who had definitely seen better days. The horse shambled over to them and seemed barely able to lift its head for Jamey's loving pat on its velvety nose.

"This is Silvester," Jamey declared, as proudly as if the animal were a prize thoroughbred.

"He's beautiful." Dorothy reached out and stroked the horse's neck. The elderly animal made the old hound look like Toto the Wonder Dog.

Jamey jumped down from the fence and began to trot toward the pigpen adjacent to the corral. "Now come meet all the pigs."

She sensed rather than heard Tom walk up behind her. "I thought you said the rest of the animals still had their teeth," she reminded him dryly.

"Oh, Silvester's got teeth, all right. Big ones. Ever heard the expression 'long in the tooth'?"

Dorothy rolled her eyes. "I imagine it was coined

just for Silvester. Tell me, do *any* of your livestock still have any life left in them?"

Tom laughed as they strolled after Jamey. "Something tells me that the pigs are going to demonstrate that to you before too long."

In the center of the pig enclosure was a building with a crudely lettered sign reading "Hog House" nailed above the door. Several pigs and hogs milled about, rooting at the ground. Jamey pointed to a young sow who waddled toward him with some effort, her abdomen ponderously close to dragging the ground.

"This is Glinda. I named her for the good witch in my favorite movie."

"Looks like Glinda's in the family way," Dorothy observed.

Tom leaned on a fence post and anchored one booted foot into a space in the pig wire. "You know what the poet said. 'In the spring a young hog's fancy turns to thoughts of love.' " Tom narrowed his green cat's eyes and gave her a wicked grin.

Jamey reached through the wire to pet the sow, and Tom quickly but gently pulled his hand away. "Remember what I told you. You're going to have to get used to not petting Glinda for a while."

Jamey looked down at his battered sneakers for a moment and then looked up at Dorothy. "Dad says that I can't pet Glinda anymore because when her pigs come, she'll be afraid I would hurt them, and she might bite me."

He gave her such a sorrowful expression that her heart went out to him. "I'm sure your dad knows best about that," she said softly. "Glinda probably appreciates you giving her a little space right now."

The little boy smiled at her, evidently pleased by her reassurance. Dorothy was struck by his responsiveness to her every kind word and gesture. He must miss his mother very much. She wondered, not for the first time since she'd been there, why Jamey was with his father and not his mother. Judges usually gave custody of young children to their mothers when a couple divorced.

"Y'know what?" Jamey's expression brightened. "Dad says that if I'm good and do all my chores that he'll let me watch Glinda have her pigs."

Dorothy stared at Tom, who was watching the pigs impassively. "You're kidding," she said flatly.

Evidently noticing the edge to her voice, Tom turned and studied her in bemusement. "No. Why? Do you have a problem with that?"

She leveled a withering glare at him, and he returned it with an even look and a raised brow. Without taking his eyes off her, he said to Jamey, "Why don't you go out to the apple tree and pick up a few apples for Glinda. I'll bet she'd like to have some."

"Good idea!" Jamey took off in the direction of the front yard, eager to get a treat for his pet.

When he was out of earshot, Dorothy said, "Are you sure you want to let a five-year-old watch the birthing process? Don't you think that's awfully . . . awfully . . ." Dorothy stammered as she searched for the right word. *"Awful?"*

"This is a farm." Tom paused for effect and his expression turned hard. "When you raise animals, nature happens, and you don't try to hide it from kids. Jamey's going to see animals born, and he's going to see them die. And guess what else? He's even going to eat a few of them."

"Oh!" Dorothy looked at him aghast.

Tom chuckled mirthlessly. "Yeah. You're a city girl all right. You probably think Big Macs grow on trees. Tom glanced at the pig lot and then back at her. The corner of his mouth quirked up lazily. "I will admit one thing, though. I'm not quite ready to explain *that* to him." Tom inclined his head toward the pigs. "Why do you think I sent him to pick up apples?"

Dorothy followed Tom's gesture and noticed for the first time that the boar was making enthusiastic romantic overtures toward one of the sows.

"Oh, my God," she said wanly. She turned back to Tom and saw that his broad, square shoulders were shaking with laughter.

"And you thought they didn't have any life in them."

Dorothy froze for a second, trying to look nonchalant, but it was no use—she could feel the blush rising toward her hairline. He leaned his huge body against the fence, his eyes half-closed with laughter but still gleaming green in the noonday sun.

"I'm going back to the house," she said, turning on her heel.

"It's time you started making lunch," he called after her. "There's some deviled ham in the pantry for sandwiches. It's pig meat, you know. After lunch we'll ask Glinda's forgiveness."

Dorothy picked up her pace, anxious to get herself out of earshot of his derisive laughter. He was without a doubt the crudest man she'd ever met. The crudest, the most confusing, exasperating, funniest, and most beautiful. He both attracted and repelled her, she realized with disgust. Had she always been this much of a goose, or was it also a result of the blow to the head? "I hope my good sense comes back with my memory," she muttered to herself.

As she stamped up the porch steps, she noticed a newspaper lying on the swing. She glanced at the date and realized with annoyance that she didn't know what today was, not the day of the month, nor of the week for that matter. But the paper had been folded tightly and looked new. Maybe it would contain some clue to her identity. And right now, finding out her identity couldn't happen soon enough for her. She had gotten the definite impression on her brief but memorable tour of the farm that Tom might be right about one thing. She was not cut out for a rural life.

She looked at the paper's masthead—*The Fairweather, Kansas, Chronicle.* "Fairweather! Ha!" she scoffed. Still reading the front page, she was headed for the door to the kitchen when her foot caught on something heavy.

"Oof!" she cried.

"Woof!" Toto responded.

She fell forward but managed to right herself before she hit the floor. "Sorry, Toto," she told the affronted dog, who stared up at her accusingly. "Sincerely. It was totally my fault. Please forgive me."

It was clear her apology failed to placate the hound, who continued to regard her with droopy, bloodshot eyes.

"I'll tell you what. If you come inside with me, I'll give you something to eat. Call it a peace offering."

She held the door open while the animal hauled itself to its feet and lumbered into the kitchen.

Still reading, she walked into the large pantry. It was today's paper all right—there was a mention of the twister she'd encountered yesterday. The tornado was reported to have torn up several acres of crops and a few houses, but caused no injuries.

"What am I? Chopped liver?" she asked the dog, and received only sullen silence in response. A mention in the paper might have given a friend or loved one an opportunity to discover where she had gone to. But this was a local paper, which meant only local people would read it. Could it be possible that she came from this area? She shuddered, even though the kitchen was toasty warm. Surely she didn't belong in this tiny backwater. It certainly didn't feel like home.

She looked away from the paper just long enough to see what was on the shelves. There were plenty of staples like macaroni and rice, along with canned goods and various kinds of supplies. She located the deviled ham and the dog food and took a can of each. After tucking a bag of chips under her arm for good measure, she went to the kitchen counter. She spread the newspaper on the counter near the can opener and continued to read, then noticed Toto again.

The dog stood motionless beside his dish, looking dubious. He'd apparently decided he would believe the stranger was going to deliver on her promise when he saw the food with his own rheumy eyes and not before.

"Hang on." Dorothy turned a page and shoved the can under the can opener while she resumed scanning the pages. When the can was open, she dumped it quickly into the dog dish and sent the empty can sailing into the trash can in the corner. Its swinging lid made a full rotation and settled back into its original position.

"Am I good, or what?"

She stopped reading long enough to locate the bread and mayonnaise and then shoved the second can under the can opener and returned her attention to the paper. Out of the corner of her eye, she noticed that Toto was exhibiting a marked enthusiasm for his food. In fact he was more animated that she'd ever seen him. Didn't they ever feed this dog?

"I guess it's true what they say about the way to a male's heart being through his stomach, huh?" The dog glanced up from his dish and gave her a look of pure devotion.

She turned another page and spread mayonnaise onto a thick slice of whole wheat bread. The newspaper hadn't offered up any clues to her identity, but there was still the classifieds, she thought hopefully as she dug into the sandwich spread with a table knife.

She finished the sandwiches while she scanned the classified ads. "There's plenty of missing dogs, cats, even pigs, but no missing people, Toto." She reached for the empty can, her eyes still glued to the fine print, and threw it into the trash. Then she refolded the news-paper and set the plate of sandwiches on the table.

Pulling out a chair for herself with one hand and reaching for the bag of chips with the other, she said, "Well, that's it. I've scoured the newspaper and there's no sign of anybody looking for me. I guess no news is good news." She sat down and munched thoughtfully on a chip. Why had she said that? She should have been disappointed she didn't find a clue to her identity in the paper.

As she pondered this, she heard Tom and Jamey climb the porch steps and enter the kitchen.

"Did the pigs like the apples you gave them?" Dorothy popped another chip into her mouth.

"Glinda and some of the others did, but two of them were too busy dancing."

Dorothy almost choked on the chip. "Dancing?" She coughed and thumped herself on the chest.

"Yeah." The boy stood on tiptoe to wash his hands at the sink. "Dad said pigs like to dance. He said they even made a movie about it—'Dances With Pigs.' "

While Jamey's back was turned, Tom gave her a lecherous grin. "Actually, I think it was called *'Dirty* Dances With Pigs.' "

"Sounds like you're not the only film buff in the family, Jamey." She arched an eyebrow at Tom.

The boy climbed into his chair and reached for the chips as Tom got them sodas from the refrigerator. "Lunch looks good," Tom said amiably.

"It's difficult to foul up sandwiches." Dorothy shrugged and picked up one of her creations. *"Bon appetit."* She took a bite and froze.

It wasn't the taste of the meat she noticed first, but the texture. She'd never felt anything quite like it—both greasy and grainy at the same time. Then there was the flavor. Tom had said they were having lean times on the farm, so she guessed he might not be able to afford the very best brands, but this stuff wasn't fit for human consumption.

"Uh-oh."

Dorothy moaned and reached for a napkin as realization dawned on her. Jamey, who was about to bite into a sandwich, stopped and looked at her questioningly. "Don't eat it!" she cried as she jumped up from the table and ran out the door to spit it out.

When she returned thirty seconds later, Tom had picked up the dog dish and was sniffing it. An open sandwich lay on his plate. "I think there's been a little mixup. Apparently it's not that difficult to foul up sandwiches after all."

Dorothy looked down at the clean linoleum floor, and at her own feet in someone else's shoes. "I've never been so embarrassed in my life."

"Come on, now." Tom set the dog dish back on the floor and put his arm loosely across her shoulders. "Don't be so hard on yourself. I'll bet when your memory comes back, you'll remember plenty of times you embarrassed yourself worse than this."

Dorothy slowly raised her gaze to meet his eyes, which were glittering with silent laughter. It was impossible not to smile. "Well, that certainly makes me feel better, you silver-tongued devil."

Tom's lips quivered slightly and his eyes danced with devilment. Jamey, still seated at the table, had begun to dissolve with laughter. The irresistible sound of his little-boy giggles and Tom's gentle squeeze of her shoulders made her feel immeasurably better. Tom began to laugh right after she did, and the three of them broke down together and laughed until their sides hurt.

During their meal of canned spaghetti and meatballs that Tom warmed in the microwave oven, Dorothy explained how the mistake came about. "I'm afraid I was trying to read the newspaper and make the sandwiches at the same time. But it was all for nothing, because there wasn't anything in the newspaper that jogged my memory or led me to believe that anybody's looking for me."

"It's early yet," Tom said. "You haven't been missing that long."

Dorothy took a sip of her soda. "That's true. Still, I was gone overnight. You would think there'd be somebody looking for me by now."

Tom put his fork down and stared at the table for a moment. "I'm sure there is. We'll keep on watching the paper and checking in with the sheriff. We'll find out who you are in no time." He rose to clear the table.

She sighed. He was back to his sweet, reassuring self. What a mercurial man he was. It was as if he'd made a decision to be indifferent, but his heart wouldn't let him be that way for long. Why would a person want to be tougher than was his nature, she wondered as she watched his broad, muscular back at the sink. Self-protection obviously. It must have hurt him terribly when his wife left.

The phone rang and she jumped. Tom answered it and Dorothy held her breath. Was it the sheriff with news? She was sure she was going to jump every time the phone rang until her memory returned or until someone found out who she was.

"Oh, yeah, Mike. Twenty minutes will be fine. We'll be ready." Tom sat back down at the table to finish his soda. "That was one of our neighbors, another farmer. He wants to borrow the bull."

She gave him a questioning look and he explained,

"Some small farmers can't afford their own bulls, so they only keep a few cows and heifers. When they need a bull, they borrow one." He took a sidelong glance at Jamey, evidently anticipating the question he knew was coming.

"Borrow one for what?" Jamey piped up, looking from Tom to Dorothy.

Dorothy looked at Tom, trying to suppress a smirk. Tom glanced at her for a moment, widening his eyes slightly. Then he turned his attention to his son, his face completely serious and matter-of-fact.

"Dancing. Mike's poor cows don't have anybody to dance with."

Dorothy held up a pair of Tom's jeans with her thumb and forefinger, trying not to touch them any more than was necessary. How did one man manage to get so dirty? It looked as if he'd taken a mud bath in them.

After lunch, she'd cleaned up the dishes while Tom went out to help load the bull into the truck for his neighbor. Two men had just driven around to the barn in a large truck with side panels. Jamey was in the house where Tom had instructed him to stay while the bull was being loaded onto the truck. The boy seemed only too happy to do this. Jamey was so attached to all the animals on the farm, usually chattering about them constantly, it made her wonder why he had never mentioned the bull.

Eager to redeem herself from the disastrous dog food incident, Dorothy had looked around for something constructive to do. The clothes washer was in the screened-

in portion of the wraparound porch next to the door to
the kitchen, as was a mound of dirty clothes and linens.
Yes, thought Dorothy. She'd do the laundry. How hard
could it possibly be?

She found that the washer already contained a freshly
washed load of clothes, so she put them in a nearby
laundry basket. The appliance was rather elderly but
seemed simple enough to operate. Just to be on the safe
side, Dorothy read the instructions on the back of the
detergent box, adding just the right amount of soap. She
loaded the washer and started it. Now there, that wasn't
too bad, she told herself. The washer made a pleasant
churning sound.

Now she'd take care of those clean clothes. She spied
a bag of clothespins hanging on the line a few yards
from the porch. After toting the basket of laundry to
the clothesline, she began to hang the clothes, shaking
out each garment so it would dry as quickly and evenly
as possible.

A sense of peace and well-being came over her as
she worked. The clothes smelled fresh and clean, like
the country air. The sun warmed her face pleasantly and
a gentle breeze lifted her hair gently off her shoulders
as she picked up a pair of Jamey's overalls—a bright
red pair. Maybe she'd been too hard on herself earlier.
Tom could be wrong about her too. She could probably
get used to this kind of life.

Her mellow mood was shattered by the shouts of men
and the sound of splintering wood.

"He's busted out of the chute!" one of the men
shouted.

"He's headed around the house!" cried another.

Dorothy froze. Was that thundering sound her heart thumping in her chest? Or, was it . . .

A bull.

The beast stopped a few yards from her and lowered its slick black head, regarding her with beady, red-rimmed eyes. It snorted once and pawed at the ground, its breath coming in hissing gasps.

Still rooted to the spot, she followed the bull's gaze to what she held in her hands—Jamey's bright red overalls, the galluses flapping gently in the breeze, their shiny metal fasteners making a faint clinking sound.

"Uh-oh."

She'd heard of out-of-body experiences. She wasn't having one of those exactly, but it did seem that all of the sudden there was only a nodding acquaintance between her mind and her body. She looked at the porch, only a few yards away, but even if she reached it, the bull could charge right up the steps with her if it wanted to.

Tom came around the corner of the house at a dead run, followed by the other two men. He stopped abruptly a few yards from the bull and the others stopped well behind him. Tom's gaze went from the bull, to the overalls, to Dorothy. She heard him mutter something under his breath.

"Don't run," he said softly.

"Don't worry." She doubted her legs would respond to such a silly idea anyway. "What's wrong with him?" she whispered. "He looks really, really . . . mad."

"He is mad. His last owner used a cattle prod to load him onto trucks. When the bull saw the loading chute, he went berserk."

"Just what I need. A thousand pounds of post-traumatic stress disorder."

The bull, evidently not one for small talk, flexed its great shoulders and began to charge. Tom swiftly moved to place himself between Dorothy and the enraged animal. His momentum caused his body to strike hers, knocking them both to the ground, but not before one of the bull's horns came into contact with his thigh. The bull trotted a few feet away, then turned. His eyes were black with menace. Dorothy knew he was going to come at them again.

She and Tom scrambled to their feet. The bull lowered its huge head and shifted its weight to its forelegs, preparing to charge.

An awful metallic noise startled them all. The bull raised its head and looked toward the porch, from where the din was coming. As the noise got steadily worse, it seemed to be accompanied by vibrations. The louder it got, the more the porch seemed to shake. It looked like the house had been seized by an earthquake.

The bull looked alternately frightened, confused, then even angrier than before. Dorothy, acting on pure instinct, hurled the overalls at the beast with all her might. The garment hit the bull squarely between the eyes with such force that each of the galluses wrapped once around the bull's horns. The rest of the material became lodged right over its eyes, effectively blinding it. It bellowed angrily, pawed the ground a few more times, and then became still.

Tom grabbed her arm and dragged her to the porch. Just then, one of the men drove up on Tom's tractor and the other produced a rope. Once up the steps and onto the porch, Dorothy looked back. The overalls covering his eyes had the same calming effect on the bull as a hood on a falcon, if only briefly. The men put the rope over its head and tied the other end to the tractor. When they started off, the bull had no choice but to lumber along behind.

"That was close," Tom breathed.

"Yes, but what's that noise?" She looked toward the awful sound and saw not a charging bull, but a charging washing machine.

Looking like some mechanical monster in a B-grade movie, the appliance skittered this way and that, rocking and clanging rhythmically as it went, its water and power connections stretched to the limit.

"Oh, no," Tom said and made a dash for it, but not before the water hose broke. A torrent of water came from each of the pipes connected to the house. Tom ran toward them, limping, turning off the washer with a slap of his hand as he sped by it. When he reached the water connections, he turned off both valves and collapsed against a wall.

"Guess I should have warned you about that spin cycle," he said breathlessly.

"Forget the spin cycle. What about the bull?" The strength was coming back into Dorothy's legs, and her heartbeat was returning to normal. Her mind was working more clearly as well, and she shuddered at the thought of how much danger they'd been in.

"That was an accident." Tom bent to examine his injured thigh. His jeans were torn slightly and blood had begun to ooze through the material.

"You're hurt!"

"It's nothing."

Dorothy heard an engine start and the truck pulled even with them on its way out of the driveway. The recalcitrant bull stood sullenly, glaring at them between two of the wooden side planks. Dorothy could swear he was plotting his revenge.

"You okay, Tom?" one of the men shouted. He tossed Jamey's overalls back onto the porch.

"Fine." Tom waved them on.

"Thanks! I'll bring him back in a few days."

"No rush," Dorothy muttered as the truck rolled away, its engine protesting the bull's weight. She retrieved the overalls and tossed them onto the stack of dirty laundry. Turning back to Tom, she said, "You'd better get out of those pants."

Tom's mouth curved upward lazily into a roguish smile. His sensual gaze took a round trip route down the length of her body and back before returning to settle on her face. "Now there's a suggestion I don't hear nearly often enough."

Dorothy shook her head. "Isn't that just like a man? Nearly killed and still can't get his mind out of the gutter."

Tom shrugged. "Danger can be very exciting, don't you think? Really gets the blood pumping."

"If you say so."

"C'mon, admit it. That run-in with the bull was the most exciting thing that's happened to you since . . ." He trailed off, evidently, remembering that he was speaking to a woman with no memory.

"Since I was nearly killed by a tornado yesterday?"

"Oh, yeah, I forgot," Tom said sheepishly. "You do lead an exciting life, don't you?"

"I can hardly wait to see what tomorrow brings. You don't have earthquakes in Kansas, do you?"

"Not that I can remember. And I think I would remember an earthquake."

"Floods?"

"Usually not."

"Hurricanes?"

"We're landlocked, remember?"

"Thank goodness for that at least. Still, at this point, I think I'm prepared to handle most anything." She thrust out her chin and set her hands on her hips in a show of bravura.

"Well, well, Miss Dorothy. I would never have figured you for the type."

She eyed him suspiciously. "What type?"

His voice, low and rough, was like the purr of a great male cat. "The type of woman who gets turned on by danger."

Five

Dorothy gave him her best no-nonsense glare, even though she could barely keep a straight face. "If that were true, I'd certainly never admit it. I'd be afraid you'd continue to sic your killer animals on me."

"You probably enjoyed the excitement with old Hickory so much, I'll bet you're going to be taking a trip to Spain to run with the bulls."

"Now, that's a lot of bull, if I've ever heard it. I assure you, I'm no daredevil. When old Hickory was about to charge, I think I would have stayed rooted to the spot if you hadn't bowled me over. My knees are still shaking."

She went over to the pile of dirty clothes and pulled out a pair of gym shorts. "Put them on."

Tom grinned and accepted the shorts. As she turned her back, he said, "Just this morning you seemed to think the animals were all old and toothless. You certainly seem to have changed your tune."

"I guess I didn't realize that before the day was out, one would actually try to kill me. Call me naive."

"You're naive," Tom said flatly.

She turned around abruptly, not bothering to ask if he was finished changing. He was. His half smile held no clue as to whether he'd been kidding or not. She opened her mouth to ask, but thought better of it. "Where's your first aid kit?" she said finally.

Tom directed her to the medicine cabinet in the downstairs bathroom. She returned with supplies to clean and bandage the wound. He'd had to remove his boots to take off his jeans, so now he lounged in one of the rockers clad in a T-shirt, skimpy gym shorts, and socks. She stopped a short way from him and had to gather her composure. Surely she'd seen a man in shorts before, but something about the way he sprawled insolently with his long, muscular legs stretched out before him made her breath catch.

When she handed him the washcloth and hydrogen peroxide, he made only a cursory dab at the wound before he started to bandage it. "Wait a minute," Dorothy said. "You've got to clean it better than that. There's no telling what kind of germs live on a bull's horns. Here, let me."

She knelt in front of him, trying to ignore the fact that he was laughing at her again.

"Good, old-fashioned dirt, that's all," he drawled. "The kind I seem to get covered with every day."

She poured a generous portion of the peroxide onto the washcloth and pressed it onto his thigh. It was difficult knowing where to look as she did so. The gym shorts were brief, well-worn, and not as roomy as they may have once been. They left little to the imagination, but that didn't stop hers from running wild.

She bit her lip and forced herself to concentrate on

his injured leg. It was easy to see that he'd once been an athlete. His legs were corded with muscle and covered with crisp black hair. She noticed a cluster of tiny scars on his knee.

"What happened here?" She pointed to the crescent-shaped group of scars.

"Old college football injury."

She capped the bottle of peroxide. "Hope it wasn't very serious."

"Serious enough to keep me from turning pro."

"I guess you were pretty disappointed." She tore off several layers of gauze for the bandage. "Most guys would kill for a chance to play professional football."

"No, not really. I've always liked living on the farm, so I didn't mind. My wife was pretty disappointed, though." He chuckled mirthlessly.

Dorothy placed the bandage on the wound and picked up the adhesive tape. "So you got married in college. That's awfully young."

"Too young. I was the college football hero with bright pro prospects and she was the head cheerleader. It was all very . . ." He looked around, as if he would see the word he was searching for painted on the porch. "Midwestern," he finally decided.

Dorothy thought she heard a hint of irony in his voice. "So you decided to come back out here where the air is clear and the living is easy."

He didn't respond right away, only looked down at her, where she still knelt at his feet. His expression was difficult to read. "You know," he said finally, "people think farm life is all fresh air and sunshine. But there's more stress involved than they realize. It either rains too much or not enough. The price of seed and fertilizer is always too high, and the price you get for your crops is always too low. The maintenance on the machinery alone . . . Well, you get the idea."

She looked at him thoughtfully as she placed adhesive tape on the edge of the bandage. "All that and then your animals try to kill you."

"Exactly," Tom said, wincing as she wound the remaining gauze around his leg. "When you have livestock, there's one crisis right after another."

Still kneeling, she gathered up the first aid supplies, preparing to take them back in the house. "You paint a depressing picture."

His expression softened as his gaze locked with hers. "It's a good life, really. But it's not for everyone. You're either cut out for it, or you're not. And if you're not, then a farm is the last place you belong."

He stood and offered his hand to help her up. She took it and allowed him to pull her to her feet, savoring the strength of his grip. She was almost to a standing position when he pulled her a little too far. She lost her balance and fell against him, her head coming down against his rock-hard chest. Her forehead brushed his chin, and she felt the light rasp of his whiskers. He smelled like clean earth.

"Sorry," he said, his voice low and resonant. "Sometimes I don't know my own strength."

You can say that again, she thought. Her knees quivering, Dorothy eased away from him and released his hand, but not before she noticed how his breathing had quickened. Standing toe to toe with him like this made her realize just how big and powerful a man he really was.

He made no move to back away from her, but stood motionless, watching her with smoky, hooded eyes.

"I'll reconnect that washer and then I'd better get back to the field."

"Okay," she said weakly.

"Poor Dorothy."

She looked up into his face and saw his mouth curve into a sympathetic smile. "What do you mean?"

He reached out and smoothed a strand of hair back from her face and let his thumb graze her cheek. "What with adventures in canine cuisine and a marauding bull and washing machine, you've had quite a day already and it's only afternoon."

Tom's warning about the hardships of life on the farm rang in her ears as his touch left a lingering trail of warmth on her cheek. She wasn't sure how far removed her real life was from the life she was leading now. So she didn't know why she should care if this man thought she was cut out for a demanding way of life. But she did care. "Don't worry about me. I'm fine." She squared her shoulders and raised her chin. "Just fine."

She'd show him she was strong. She had no idea if she *was* strong and independent, but suddenly she wanted to be. Because of his kindness to her, she wanted to be someone Tom could count on.

Dorothy busied herself the rest of the afternoon with light chores like sweeping and dusting. She considered trying her hand at vacuuming, but decided to save that for another day. She wouldn't press her luck with machines anymore this afternoon.

When Jamey went out to feed the chickens, she gathered in the laundry, folded it neatly, and took it upstairs in the basket. She put the folded towels and washcloths in the hall linen closet, then pushed open the door to Jamey's room and placed his small stack of clothing on his bed. Putting down the basket, she looked around her and sighed. It was such a sweet room for a little boy. The bed was neatly made, but toys, mostly cars and trucks, were spread across the floor.

A half-finished model airplane sat on a child-sized desk beside a couple of framed photographs. She walked over to the desk and picked up one of the photos, a five-by-seven shot of a young Tom in his football uniform. The photo looked like a projection of what Jamey would look like in a few years. She set the photo down and picked up the other. The glamorous studio portrait was of a young woman with lustrous blonde hair and heavily made up blue eyes. She was strikingly pretty, beautiful even, Dorothy allowed. This was not Tom's sister, whose photo Dorothy had seen last night. It had to be Margaret, Jamey's mother.

The woman's expression was full of youthful confidence, almost cockiness. It was the face of a woman who knew that the world was hers for the taking. A face that belonged at debutante balls and country clubs. A fresh-faced farm girl she was not. She could see why Tom must have fallen in love with her, though. She had the face any man could fall in love with, and probably a figure to match. Dorothy sighed and set the frame back on the desk, then looked at Tom's picture once more.

His expression was sunny and carefree, so different

from the troubled look she'd seen on his face at times. She thought again of what he'd said about the rigors of life on the farm and wondered if that was what had changed him over the years. She closed the door to Jamey's room and entered Tom's, somewhat guiltily, even though she had a perfectly acceptable reason to be there.

She put the stack of laundry on the bed, a beautiful, king-sized four-poster with an ornately carved head-board. She sat down on the bed and reached out with both hands, running her palms across the quilt, feeling the varying textures of its different fabrics.

There was a bookshelf, a chest of drawers, and a dresser, each with its share of masculine knickknacks— a pocket knife, nail clippers, a money clip. There were two photos of Jamey, one as an infant and another more recent one. Except for the pictures of his son, it was the austere bedroom of a bachelor.

There was no photo of his ex-wife. There were no lingering feminine touches in his bedroom. No lace curtains, only plain beige ones. No fluffy throw pillows, no doily on the dresser. What had this room looked like when Margaret was the woman of the house? How much trouble had he gone to in order to purge any trace of her from his room, any reminder of her presence in his life? Reminders of her must be very painful for him. He must have loved her very much.

He hadn't said much about her; that was, he hadn't said much about her *directly.* But Dorothy had the feeling that some of the remarks he'd made had something to do with Margaret and her life here. For example, his lecture on the challenges of farm life came directly after his remark about having gotten married too young.

And then there was his admission that his wife was disappointed about his not becoming a professional athlete. Just how disappointed had she been about coming to live on the farm instead of being the wife of an NFL star?

And there was something else—yesterday's story about the farmer whose wife was desperately unhappy. Had he been talking about himself and Margaret? Was Margaret the rich city girl for whom life on the farm had been a misery? That would explain their divorce, and it would also certainly explain his reaction to the theory that she herself was wealthy and from the city. Was he projecting his wife's problems onto her?

She looked out the window at the late afternoon sun. She would have to go back to the kitchen soon and see what she could make for dinner. She didn't relish the prospect, given the way her culinary skills had manifested themselves at lunch, but that was one horse she was going to have to get back on, and soon.

She was suddenly struck by a wave of dizziness, accompanied by a pain where her head injury had been. She had to rest, if only for a few minutes, before she did anything. Just a little catnap and she would resume her work.

So with the stack of Tom's clothing on one side of her and the laundry basket on the other, she stretched out sideways on the bed. Her mind returned to her situation with Tom. If he was, as she suspected, prejudiced against her because of problems he'd had with his wife, that was patently unfair. She'd just have to prove to him that she was different from Margaret. Of course, she probably wouldn't be here long enough to make much of an impression, but she'd do what she could. It was the principle of the thing.

She'd just close her eyes and rest for a moment, that was all.

Tom walked to the door of his bedroom and drew up short. Jamey had told him that Dorothy was asleep on his bed, but nothing had prepared him for the sight of her there. His body sagged against the door frame, all the strength having gone suddenly out of his legs. She was stretched out on her back, her honey-brown hair catching the last of the sun's rays from the window. Her lips were parted slightly as if in invitation to a kiss, and her breasts rose and fell in a rhythm he found mesmerizing.

He fought the urge to lie beside her, cover her mouth with his own and her body with his. He drew a hand across his mouth and cursed himself savagely. This afternoon he'd almost gone wild with her touching his thigh, and now she was on his bed looking like every man's dream. What had he been thinking in letting her come here? He'd always thought of himself as a man with self-control, but if he were able to keep his hands off her for another day, it would be a miracle.

He straightened when he heard Jamey's footsteps on the stairs. "Who's that sleeping in my bed?" Tom said with a wink at his son.

Dorothy's consciousness was pierced by the rumbling of low, masculine laughter combined with a run of high-pitched staccato giggles. She sat bolt upright. "Who? What?"

"It's Goldilocks! And she's still here!" Tom pointed an accusing finger at her and then set both hands on his hips, his eyes glittering with mischief.

Jamey flung himself on the bed beside her, scattering the stack of clothing she'd folded. "I'm Baby Bear," he shouted between giggles.

She smoothed down her hair and looked around sheepishly. "I was putting the laundry away and I just thought I'd rest for a minute." She looked at the alarm clock on Tom's bedside table and groaned. It was six-thirty. "Oh, no. I was going to make dinner."

"Don't worry. When we found you up here, we decided to take care of dinner and let you sleep until it was ready. Come on down after you freshen up, and we'll eat."

He reached out to help her up, and she took his hand. As his broad hand closed over her own, she was hit with the same intimate shock of sensation she got every time he touched her. He pulled her up as if she were no heavier than a rag doll, and when she was on her feet, she was close enough to feel the warmth his body radiated.

He didn't release her hand right away, but massaged her palm in a circular motion with the pad of his thumb. The seductive gesture made her whole body throb like a tuning fork, and she suppressed a gasp. When she looked into his eyes, she saw they were no longer filled with amusement, but with such virile intensity that heat rose to her face.

"So what are we having?" She tried to sound nonchalant and hoped her eyes didn't betray her state of mind.

"Porridge!" Jamey cried, and collapsed into a fit of giggles once more.

Jamey's "porridge" turned out to be a very tasty beef and vegetable stew that Tom had thrown together. Tom entertained Jamey with the tale of his and Dorothy's close encounter with Hickory the bull, heavily embellished with heroism on both their parts.

"And then, right before he was about to charge, Dorothy used your red overalls to blind that old bull. She just threw them at him and they got caught on his horns. They hung down in front of his eyes so he couldn't see."

"Wow!" Jamey said, clearly impressed. "Dorothy, did you really do that?"

"Sure did. But it was your dad who knocked me out of Hickory's path and saved me."

Jamey looked at both of them with awe. Evidently Hickory was the one animal on the farm to whom Jamey was willing to give all the space he wanted.

"Is he always that dangerous?" she asked Tom.

"No, not really. Unfortunately, he'd gotten all riled up with us trying to make him go up the loading chute. But even on a good day, I'd give him a wide berth."

"Don't worry. I will."

After supper, they all retired to the living room, where Tom excused himself to resume his paperwork and Jamey turned on his favorite video. This must be their nightly routine, Dorothy figured.

"I'd like to look at some of your books, if you don't mind," she said.

"Sure. Help yourself."

With Tom absorbed in bookkeeping and Jamey glued to the television, Dorothy examined the shelves of books. The agriculture texts didn't interest her much, but the mystery novels looked enticing. She resisted the temptation to indulge in the mysteries, because she wasn't interested in passing the time. She needed something that might help jog her memory. After a minute or two, she found just what she needed—the encyclopedia.

Might as well begin at the beginning, she thought, and reached for the first volume. As she returned to the sitting area, she saw Tom glance at her from the corner of his eye, evidently curious as to what she had selected. Somehow pleased by this, she sat down in an overstuffed armchair.

She didn't know precisely what she was looking for. She only hoped that perhaps the words or pictures would strike a spark of familiarity. Maybe something would remind her of what she did for a living, or of some favorite possession or activity. She began flipping through the pages. She was pretty sure she wasn't an aardvark trainer or abacus saleswoman. Diving for abalone sounded like fun, but didn't ring a bell. She didn't think she could play the accordion, at least she hoped not.

She continued to turn the pages rapidly until she reached a listing headed "Amnesia." The initial definition read: "Loss of memory, usually due to brain injury, neurological illness, shock, fatigue, or repression."

Dorothy frowned, unconsciously rubbing the spot on her forehead where she'd received the worst blow in the accident. The lump that had formed there had almost vanished, and the bruise that was left was beginning to fade. But could she have sustained a brain injury? Probably not. All the tests they ran on her in the hospital would have turned up something if she had received an injury like that.

If her case of amnesia was caused by only the minor bump she had sustained, why had her memory not returned when her injury healed? The doctor had assured her that she had sustained no permanent damage. She looked again at the list of possible causes. They wouldn't have released her from the hospital if she was suffering from shock, and surely all those tests would have turned up any neurological problems. She didn't feel particularly fatigued, so that left only one remaining cause—repression.

She closed the encyclopedia as a new and disturbing thought occurred to her. Was it possible that her amnesia was all in her mind? Was there something so terrible about her former life that her mind refused to return to it? Was the sheriff right about her being some sort of criminal? It couldn't be—it just couldn't.

"You okay? You don't look well." The voice was soft, gentle, and a bit tentative. It was the voice of a man sensitive enough to know that sometimes a kind word can push a woman over the brink of emotion faster than a harsh one.

Dorothy sat up straight in her chair. "Yes. Fine. I was just looking through the encyclopedia for anything that might jog my memory." She laughed a little. "I know it's silly, but I guess a long shot is better than no shot at all."

"It doesn't sound silly," he said easily. "It sounds perfectly logical to me."

He looked at her with sympathy and a bit of humor. She rewarded him with a smile of gratitude, and he returned to his work. She gazed at him a moment longer, as long as she dared. Once again he'd managed to share his strength with her. Although he could be harsh sometimes, he seemed to sense her low points, the times she needed encouragement, and he'd managed to make her feel better.

She returned to the bookshelves and replaced Volume A. While she debated starting on another volume, her gaze strayed to a nearby book with a colorful binding. She slid the book off the shelf and opened it—it was a college yearbook. On the first page was a black-and-white photograph of the entrance to a university.

A jolt of recognition shot through her. She splayed her fingers across the photo as if she could feel it, absorb it through her skin. She knew this place, knew it well. She turned the pages eagerly, but none of the other campus photos sparked the same familiarity.

"Do you have any more yearbooks from this university?"

Tom looked up from his work. "No. But I think my sister has some. She went to college there too. Why? Do you see something familiar?"

"There's something about this scene. I know I've seen it before, but none of the other photos of the campus rings a bell like this one."

Tom looked at her hopefully. "So do you think you went to that university?"

"Could be." Dorothy returned to the easy chair with the yearbook. "Or it could be a fluke. Maybe I just saw it on the news or something."

Tom stroked his chin. "I'd say you and I are about the same age. It's possible we were in school at the same time. See if your photograph's in there."

"Right." Could it be that her name was somewhere in the pages of this book? Eagerly, she turned to the class photos and began scanning the portraits of every woman in each class, page by page.

"Two pairs of eyes are better than one."

Dorothy looked up to see that Tom had come to look over her shoulder. He rested his forearm along the top of the easy chair behind her head and leaned over her. A tingle tightened her scalp as his chin brushed the side of her head, and she breathed in his clean, masculine scent.

Together, they examined all the photos. When they reached the end, Dorothy snapped the book closed, resisting the urge to throw it across the room. Tom put a reassuring hand on her shoulder.

"Tell you what. I'll call my sister and ask her to drop off those other yearbooks the next time she's out this way. In fact, she probably wouldn't mind making a special trip."

"Thanks. That would be great." Dorothy took a deep breath and let Tom take the book from her and replace it on the shelf. She'd felt so close—so close to finding out what her name was, where she belonged. She could almost taste it. There was a definite connection with that university.

She'd been so absorbed in her search that she'd forgotten about Jamey, and it was past his bedtime. He was asleep on the couch, the remote control propped on his knee. With his usually animated face relaxed and peaceful and his eyelashes curling on his cheek, he looked even more angelic than when he was awake. She felt a deep pang within herself, something painful and sweet at the same time. Something downright maternal, she thought. But what woman wouldn't feel that way about such a sweet, loving child?

Tom turned off his desk lamp and then the television set before he went to Jamey's side. With a deftness obviously derived from practice, he lifted the boy into his arms so gently that the child didn't even stir.

"You did that very nicely," Dorothy said softly.

Tom grinned. "When I was a football player they said I had soft hands. I'm glad they're good for more than just receiving passes."

She had to bite her tongue to keep from making a corny joke about how good they might be for *making* passes. She thought back to the times he'd taken her hand in his. His touch had been an irresistible combination of gentleness and strength. It made her wonder what the rest of him would feel like. "I think I'll turn in too. It's been a rough day."

Tom, who had turned toward the stairs with Jamey, laughed softly. "That's an understatement. You should have seen your face when you realized what was in that sandwich."

She laughed. "You should have seen *your* face when you realized your bull was about to kill me."

At the top of the stairs, Tom paused by the door to Jamey's room as Dorothy came up beside him. Even in the near darkness of the hallway, she could see the light of laughter in his eyes. "Look on the bright side. Tomorrow's another day. And it can't possibly be as bad as this one."

The next morning after breakfast, while Tom was in the field and Jamey was busy feeding the animals, Dorothy stood staring numbly at the dust motes dancing in the streamers of light from the windows. The dust floated through the air and settled all around her—and on her. Under different circumstances, they might even have been pretty, she thought with a kind of out-of-body remoteness.

"It exploded," she muttered to herself. "The bastard actually exploded on me. That's the last time I look into the south end of a northbound vacuum cleaner."

She checked her reflection in the ornate mirror that hung by the door. Her head and shoulders were covered with hunks of dust and dirt and a few bits of string. A slight movement directed her gaze upward. A single pillow feather had caught a draft of air and was making a lazy, zig-zagging descent. She followed it with her eyes until it settled on top of her head as a finishing touch.

She sneezed violently and looked down at the ancient canister vacuum on the floor. It was silver and was shaped, appropriately enough, like a bomb. The back of the thing was halfway open, revealing a torn and over-flowing bag.

"I see Tom let the bag get too full again," said a voice from behind her.

Dorothy jumped and turned around. She saw a pretty, dark-haired woman coming toward her from the dining room. Dorothy's heart leapt for a moment—the woman was familiar! Then she realized why. This attractive young woman with the laughing green eyes was Tom's sister—the girl she'd seen in the family photo.

"You poor thing. That worthless old piece of junk should have been replaced years ago." She held out her hand. "I'm Casey, Tom's sister. He phoned me this morning and told me all about you."

Dorothy smiled and shook her hand, noticing for the first time that the woman carried two books. "I'm afraid there's not much to tell." She felt a flutter of excitement as she eyed the yearbooks.

Casey held out the books. "Maybe we can fix that. But first, let's try to get some of the dust and dirt off of you. You look like a giant dust bunny."

After Casey helped Dorothy shake most of the dirt off her clothing and out of her hair, the two women sat on the sofa together and looked through the college yearbooks Casey had brought. Dorothy's frustration mounted as she turned page after page without seeing a photo of herself, or of anything that seemed familiar at all.

Dorothy closed the last book and handed it to Casey, then jammed her hands through her hair in frustration. "I guess you've come all the way out here on a wild goose chase. I'm sorry to have put you to the trouble."

She hung her head and tried to compose herself. She'd felt as if she were so close to a memory about that university.

Casey patted her arm sympathetically and placed the books on the coffee table. "It was no trouble at all. I like to come by and check on Tom and Jamey every week or two anyway, and I haven't been here lately. I'm glad they have you to take care of them, even if it's just for a little while. Now I won't worry so much."

Dorothy laughed dryly. "You've got to be kidding. So far I've almost poisoned them and destroyed most of their major appliances. And I've only been here two days. The only thing I seem to be good for is comic relief."

"That alone is worth more than you know."

Dorothy watched Casey as the younger woman stood and walked to the bay windows. Her smile was tinged with regret.

"What do you mean?" Dorothy asked.

"When Tom told me on the phone about your run-in with the washing machine and the bull, well, it was the first time I'd heard him laugh that way in . . ."

"A year?" Dorothy finished Casey's sentence, remembering what Tom had said about Margaret's having left him about a year ago.

Casey looked at her pointedly. "Much longer than that." She looked out the window again and rested her hand lightly on her abdomen, the way only a pregnant woman does. Dorothy felt like a dolt for being so wrapped up in her own problems that she didn't notice Casey's condition until now. She had often heard the old saying that pregnant women had a glow about them.

She'd always thought it was just so much talk until she looked closely at Tom's sister.

"I want Tom to be happy, as happy as I am." Casey continued thoughtfully. "He hasn't been in a long, long time, and he deserves to be."

Dorothy was curious about her reference to Tom's unhappiness but decided it would be rude to press for more information. Instead, she only managed to stammer, "He's so—that is, well, he seems like a wonderful man."

"He is. I wouldn't want to see him hurt again for anything in the world." Casey gave her another meaningful look.

Dorothy shifted uncomfortably. She'd only known Tom a couple of days. Did his sister think she had designs on him? "Well, I, I mean, of course you wouldn't want to see him hurt, and I'm sure—"

"He likes you. I can tell." Casey leaned against the wall. "And unless I miss my guess, you're very fond of him."

Dorothy blinked in astonishment. "How do you—how do you know I'm fond of him?"

"I used to stammer like that when I talked about my husband, Ned." A contented glow came to the cheeks of the farm wife. "Sometimes I still do."

"Well, I—what I mean to say is, that I—" She was stammering again and Casey was laughing. This whole family was so . . . exasperating. She paused to gather her thoughts, and then continued. "Tom is a great guy, but sometimes he's so preoccupied, so intense even. He's not the easiest man to get to know."

Casey's face grew serious. It was a look Dorothy had

seen at times on her brother's face—a drawing together of dark brows, a shadow over green eyes. "Yes, that's true." She walked back to the couch and sat down beside Dorothy again. "I'll tell you something about my brother. Something important."

Six

"What I want you to know is this. No matter how gruff my brother sometimes seems on the outside, he's actually one of the most sensitive men you'll ever know. He feels things more deeply than most people."

Dorothy didn't know what to say, but she was curious to know all about Tom. Perhaps with a little encouragement, Casey would give her some insights into what made Tom tick. "I sense that Tom has been really hurt in the past, but naturally, I haven't asked him about it. I assume it has something to do with the breakup of his marriage . . ." Dorothy waited to see if Casey would volunteer any information.

Casey nodded and settled back against the sofa's patchwork pillows. She reopened one of the yearbooks to a page of homecoming photos. In the middle of the layout was a picture of Tom and Margaret, she with a tiara and sash—homecoming queen. Of course, thought Dorothy. Who else? She looked absolutely golden.

Casey looked at the image of her brother's smiling face and sighed. "Tom's marriage was not a happy one. It hurt to see him so miserable."

The back door slammed and the sound of two sets of footsteps made their way toward them, the lighter ones going double time. Dorothy sighed. She'd missed her window of opportunity to find out more about Tom. Jamey rounded the corner toward them at his usual breakneck speed.

"Aunt Casey, Dorothy's going to be taking care of me."

Casey reached out and hugged the boy. "And I know she's going to do a great job."

Dorothy shrugged. "At the rate I'm going, Jamey could do a better job taking care of me."

Tom had stopped when he came to the vacuum cleaner and was looking down at it. "Oops," he said.

"Oops is right." Casey gave him an accusing look. "You forgot to warn her about that prehistoric vacuum just like you forgot to warn her about the washing machine's spin cycle and the bull."

"I know. Sorry."

His contrite grin had probably gotten him out of his share of scrapes with females, but his sister was unaffected. "What Tom means," Casey said, turning to Dorothy, "is that these things were just as much his fault as yours and you're not to feel bad about them."

"Well, there *was* the dog food," he offered.

"Tom!"

"Only kidding. Casey's right. I should have warned you about these things."

Dorothy laughed, amused by the brother-and-sister act and grateful for Casey's efforts to lift her spirits.

Casey ruffled Jamey's hair and said, "Well, I've got to go. I need to run my errands in town and get back to the farm." She rose and Dorothy followed her past where Tom knelt over the metal carcass of the vacuum cleaner, to the front door. They stepped outside onto the front porch. "Remember what I told you," Casey said.

Dorothy watched Casey get into her truck and waved as she started down the driveway. She decided that she liked Casey very much. The young woman had her brother's kindness and humor. She probably had his intensity as well. Perhaps she'd get another opportunity to draw her out about Tom's background. Not that Tom's life history was any of her business, of course.

Jamey announced that he was going outside to play with Toto. Dorothy closed the door after him and looked down at Tom, tinkering with the vacuum. "Is it dead?"

He looked at her incredulously. "Of course not. This is a great machine, a classic. They don't make them like this anymore."

"Something tells me there's a reason for that, don't you think?"

"Not at all. They don't make '57 Chevys anymore either, but . . ." His voice trailed off as his train of logic jumped the track.

She nudged it with her toe. "It's not moving."

"It's got plenty of life left in it." Tom stood up and put his arm around her shoulder, giving her a little squeeze. With a grin worthy of a used car salesman, he said, "Trust me."

"Great. What do you want for lunch?"

He looked down at her as they walked toward the kitchen and asked warily, "What do you recommend?"

"I make a mean tuna sandwich."

"How do you know?"

It was a fair question. She didn't know how she knew, she just did. Reaching up, she pulled down on the bill of his cap until it almost covered his eyes. "Trust me."

The next morning, Dorothy sat at the kitchen table, carefully reading the morning paper for any news that might offer a clue to her identity. Tom had checked in with the sheriff, who was as baffled as ever, but vowed once again to solve the case or, as he put it, "die trying." She shivered. Tom had also made her an appointment with his family doctor for the following week. Her amnesia had already lasted longer than the emergency room physician had predicted, so as a precaution, she'd agreed to see another doctor.

While Tom had continued with his planting, she had made hours worth of phone calls to various organizations and government agencies to research any clues to her identity. While she had spoken to many sympathetic people, none of them were able to come up with any useful information. A local librarian had even agreed to do an Internet search for anyone who might have reported a woman of her description missing. After a few hours, the woman had called to say that she'd been unable to turn up anything, even after searching all existing databases on missing persons.

Determined to take her mind off her mounting frustration, she decided to distract herself by cleaning the kitchen. After mopping the floor and cleaning the counters, the next order of business was to wash a load of dishes in the dishwasher. After she'd loaded the breakfast dishes into the machine, Dorothy stood back and surveyed her work. Plastic cups in the top as Tom had instructed. Pots and pans on the bottom. Nothing could be easier. She'd show him she had sense enough to work a major appliance.

When she opened the cupboard under the sink and removed the box of dishwasher detergent, she saw that it was nearly empty. A quick check of the pantry revealed that there was no new box.

There was, however, a fresh box of laundry detergent.

Dorothy took the cheery orange box off the shelf and glanced at the back. Drawings showed the different uses for the soap. A drawing of sparkling clean dishes in a dish drainer caught her eye. Excellent, she thought. Since it was clearly safe for dishes, she'd just use some of the laundry soap in the dishwasher.

She emptied the last tiny bit of the dish detergent into the soap receptacle on the dishwasher and filled it the rest of the way with laundry soap. Then she fastened the door and pressed the button.

With a sense of satisfaction, she looked around her at the clean kitchen. Everything sparkled, except for Toto of course, who napped silently on the linoleum in the far corner of the room. Even Toto didn't look that bad, but then she was in a good mood. Nothing was going to go wrong today. No way, no how. All was right with the world.

After a morning's work, she figured she deserved a short coffee break before preparing lunch. She poured herself a cup from the coffeemaker and went out onto the porch to enjoy the perfect spring morning, letting the screen door shut behind her. She dropped into the comfy rocking chair next to the porch railing and propped her elbows on the generous armrests. Swaying gently, she breathed in the country-fresh air and let the warmth of the sun caress her cheek.

The only sounds she heard were the chirps of the birds, the lazy squeak of the weathervane in the gentle breeze, and the "swishing" sound of the dishwasher . . . and the faraway whine of Toto, probably having another one of his dreams.

Jamey, who'd been visiting the animals, came to the edge of the porch. "Glinda's even bigger today. I'll bet she's going to have a hundred babies."

Dorothy smiled. "For Glinda's sake, Jamey, I hope you're wrong."

Suddenly, the screen door banged open and Toto skidded out onto the porch. Dorothy saw him out of the corner of her eye and did a double take. He was enveloped in a cloud of soapsuds that seemed to have a life of its own.

Dorothy sprang from the rocker and joined Jamey, whose eyes had grown as round as saucers, at the kitchen door. The kitchen looked like a winter wonderland, with fluffy soapsuds piled up like drifting snow in the kitchen floor—and spreading.

"Wow," Jamey said reverently. "Cool."

"Quick, Jamey, go hose off Toto. Be sure to get any soap out of his eyes."

Jamey did as he was told, leading Toto by the collar down the porch steps to the spigot. Dorothy entered the kitchen, lost her footing, and slipped over to the dishwasher. She managed to get it turned off, and she swabbed out the remainder of the soap suds that filled the dishwasher's cavity.

As she swept the suds out the door with the biggest broom she could find, she cursed herself. She had used her best judgment to cope with the soap situation, and her best judgment hadn't been good enough. Every time she thought she had a handle on housekeeping, she'd been proven emphatically, humiliatingly wrong.

Jamey joined her again, tiptoed through the suds to the pantry, and returned with some towels. As he began to mop up the soap on all fours, he said, "You used laundry soap in the dishwasher, didn't you?"

"How'd you know?" Great. Even a five-year-old child had more sense about domestic chores than she did.

"Dad did the same thing once."

Suddenly she felt much better. "He did?"

"Yeah." Jamey wrung out a towel in the sink and then started mopping again. "It says on the back that you can use it for dishes, but it's just for using in the sink. That's what he figured later anyway."

"So what did you do?"

"Well, we body surfed for a while. Then we cleaned up like we're doing now."

Dorothy laughed out loud at the mental picture of Tom and Jamey sliding through the soapy kitchen. "I wish I could have seen that. You know what, Jamey, how about we keep this little mistake of mine just between us?"

The boy smiled. "Okay."

Jamey was so much his father's son. Just as Tom could usually think of something to say to make her feel better about her situation, so could Jamey in his own way.

When they'd gotten things to rights, Dorothy gave

Jamey a chocolate soda and went into the pantry to figure out what they could have for lunch. On the top shelf, she saw a gingham-lined picnic basket and an idea came to her. The kitchen would still take a while to completely dry. "Hey, Jamey, where would be a good place for a picnic?"

Jamey looked up from his soda with interest. "The apple tree down by the creek. Under there would be good."

"Sounds perfect. Why don't you walk out to the field where your dad is working and tell him to meet us under the apple tree at noon."

Tom jumped down from the tractor and threw his work gloves into the cab. Jamey had said that Dorothy wanted him to be at the apple tree next to the creek at noon.

He sank down onto the grass under the tree and leaned back against its gnarled trunk, propping his forearms on his updrawn knees. Closing his eyes, he imagined he was a boy again, riding his horse bareback in this very pasture.

The thought of memories made him think of Dorothy, who had none. *Dorothy*. He'd opened up a serious can of worms when he'd allowed her to come stay with him and Jamey. Would anyone ever come for her? Would her memory return? What if it didn't?

Tom heard his son's voice first and then Dorothy's, far away, riding to him on the breeze a little at a time. They were coming across the pasture toward him, with Toto ambling along behind. Dorothy carried a large basket. Tom made no move to stand up, but remained motionless, letting himself enjoy the sight of his smiling son and his beautiful companion.

She tilted her head back and laughed at something Jamey said as she moved gracefully through the lush green grass and colorful wildflowers. The scene, washed bright by last night's rain, reminded him of the first time he'd seen her, laying in her car on the edge of a field of poppies. Only now she seemed strong and more confident, instead of helpless and frightened. He felt pure, simple joy just watching her move.

The midday sun filtered through the boughs of the tree, and ribbons of it shone on the golden highlights of her honey-brown hair. He wanted to say something meaningful and charming. But whatever wit he possessed had deserted him under the gaze of her cornflower blue eyes.

"So, what's in the basket?" he said when they reached his side.

"A picnic." She set the basket on the ground and spread a red-and-white checkered tablecloth in front of Tom. He followed her every move as she set out paper plates, napkins, and containers of food. When Dorothy finally sat down opposite him in the grass, she did so daintily, and looked around herself carefully, as if she expected a horde of bugs to invade her space at any moment. He bit his lip to keep from grinning.

Dorothy removed a quart jar of lemonade from the basket and filled three plastic cups as she recounted her morning of fruitless research. It sounded as if she was trying to keep the frustration out of her voice.

Dorothy handed Jamey a paper plate and a small plastic bag of kibble. "Why don't you feed Toto this? Take it a little ways away so he won't be tempted to beg for a sandwich while we're eating." Jamey ran to do as he was told and Dorothy began opening the containers of food.

"I'm sorry you didn't have any luck," Tom said softly, watching her. He wondered if she could tell that he wasn't sorry at all.

She looked up and smiled. "Thanks." She stared off into the distance and looked as if she wanted to say something more, but stopped.

"What?" he prompted.

"Oh, nothing."

"No, really. What were you going to say?"

She took a small sip of the lemonade before she began. "Even though housework doesn't seem to come naturally to me, taking care of Jamey does. I've been wondering . . . what if I'm a mother? What if I have a child of my own out there somewhere? A child who needs me."

Tom fiddled with his glass uneasily. "If you were a mother, don't you think you'd sense it somehow?" The turn of conversation made him uncomfortable.

Dorothy looked thoughtful as she put potato salad on the plates. "Maybe you're right. If I was a mother, I think I would sense it more strongly, amnesia or no amnesia. All I have now is a vague sense that it might be possible." She sat back on her heels and looked across the expanse of blue sky, her eyes still vaguely troubled. "But then when I look at Jamey, I . . . I just don't know."

Tom swirled his glass of lemonade and glanced at

Jamey and Toto playing chase. This talk of Dorothy's other life, her real life, had begun to put a damper on the good mood she had inspired in him. "What about the thing we talked about the other day?" He could barely make himself say it. "The thing about the missing ring? Do you have any feelings about that now that you've had time to think about it?"

Dorothy shrugged. "Not really. I have no idea if I'm married or engaged."

Tom exhaled slowly, realizing that he'd been holding his breath for her reply. He felt uneasy, having been reminded of the tenuous nature of his and Jamey's relationship with Dorothy. At least Jamey was happy for now. He came racing back and accepted his plate of picnic fare with enthusiasm.

"What's for dessert?" Jamey asked after he'd wolfed down his sandwich.

Dorothy held out a plastic bowl to him. "Grapes."

The boy looked a little disappointed but accepted the grapes and munched on some of them thoughtfully. He looked overhead at the canopy of branches and the fruit they bore. "I wish we had apple pie."

"That's his favorite," Tom explained, helping himself to some grapes from the bowl. "He could probably eat a whole one by himself if I let him."

"Well, maybe I'll just make you one some day soon."

Tom tried to stifle a smirk, but it was too late.

"What was that look for? Don't you believe I can bake a pie?" She gave him a challenging look, one brow raised.

"It's just that baking is a little tougher than regular cooking, that's all."

"Is that so? Well when I bake that pie, it might not be a thing of beauty, but at least it won't have any dog food in it."

Tom and Jamey laughed. Tom decided he was going to have to learn not to suggest that she couldn't do something, because if he did, she was going to bust a gut trying to do it. He was beginning to realize what a determined woman she was.

He changed the subject, launching into a series of fanciful stories of his exploits as a young man. Jamey rolled his eyes comically at the more unbelievable parts.

"Dad. C'mon. You didn't *really* hunt buffalo in this very field."

Tom feigned dismay. "What's this? My son doesn't believe his own father? Now, that's a sad commentary on the youth of today. Why, I'll bet if you go on down to that stream, you'll find some buffalo tracks right now."

Jamey giggled and went to join Toto, who was drinking noisily from the stream. "How will I be able to tell the difference between cow tracks and buffalo tracks?" he called over his shoulder.

Tom looked quickly to Dorothy for help.

She shook her head and took another sip of lemonade. "You're on your own, buffalo boy."

"Ah, let's see." Tom scratched his head. "Buffalo tracks are bigger."

"Old Hickory's tracks are pretty big," Jamey called back, still skeptical.

"You won't see his tracks. I don't keep him in this pasture."

"Oh, yeah. I forgot."

They watched Jamey in silence for a while. Then Dorothy leaned back, propped on one elbow, and regarded Tom thoughtfully. "Those were quite some exploits you had there, cowboy. Who knew wild Indians were roaming these very plains as recently as the seventies?"

"A little-known historical fact."

"Mmm hmm." She sighed and squinted up into the sunlight.

She stretched out full-length, now apparently oblivious to the threat of bugs, and put her hands behind her head, her fingers linked. For the first time since she'd come to the farm, she appeared relaxed, and he was happy for that. But the way she looked lying there in the grass, her hair fanning out around her like a halo, her womanly curves on tantalizing display, did little to relax *him*. His body tensed in ways it hadn't done in a long time.

"I guess I'll have to do that," she said.

"Chase Indians across the plains? It'd be considered a little unorthodox nowadays. I mean, most women would just settle for aerobics."

The apple she threw bounced neatly off his shoulder. "I mean, make up some good stories about my own background. In case my memory doesn't come back, at least I'd have something I could impress people with."

Tom smiled, pleased that she could joke about her memory never returning when only yesterday she'd been distraught about that possibility. Maybe Jamey was as good for her as she was for Jamey. And it might even be that if he could keep his foot out of his mouth, *he* could be good for her too. How about that? Tom

Weaver, a positive influence on a woman. He supposed there was a first time for everything.

"Good idea," he said. "What, for instance?"

"I don't know. You're the storyteller. What do you suggest?"

"Hmmm." Tom thought a minute. "How about royalty? If you're going to make up a story about your background, you might as well make it a good one, right?"

"I like it already." Dorothy rolled onto her stomach and rested her chin on her crossed arms.

"You're a princess," Tom said.

"I beg your pardon?" She narrowed her eyes at him.

He laughed. "No, no. I mean a *real* princess. And you come from a country where everyone's beautiful."

Dorothy sniffed. "I'll bet you say that to all the princesses."

Tom reached for the plastic bowl of grapes and dumped its remaining contents onto the tablecloth. Placing the bowl on Dorothy's head, he said with authority, "I hereby pronounce you Princess Dorothy of the Netherlands, here on a diplomatic, er, culture exchange."

Dorothy laughed, causing the bowl to fall off. "So what about my prince?" She rolled onto her back again and closed her eyes, as if imagining herself in the identity Tom had just created for her.

"Prince?"

"I've *got* to have a prince." She covered her mouth as she yawned, and let her hand drop back down to the grass. "Does he love me very much?"

Since her eyes were closed, Tom let his gaze boldly

travel from one end of her body and back again. "Oh, yes." The urge to touch her was overwhelming.

The corners of her mouth turned gently upward. "Tell me more."

He did. He told her of mountains her prince would climb, rivers he would swim, and dragons he would slay, all for her. He told her story after story, stopping only when the rhythm of her breathing told him she was asleep.

Seven

"Did you want something else, Miss?" The old man behind the counter looked at her cautiously, as if he expected her to rob him at gunpoint. She stifled a burst of nervous laughter. The man, slowly drying a parfait glass with a rag, reminded her of an Old West bartender, with his bushy gray mustache and eyebrows.

But instead of a ten-gallon hat, he wore the white uniform of a soda jerk. And instead of a saloon bar, he stood behind the old-fashioned chrome-and-formica lunch counter of a drugstore. She had an overpowering urge to call out, "Whiskey!" Instead, she said, "No, thanks."

Dorothy fidgeted with the straw in her milk shake. She glanced over her shoulder at three middle-aged women in a booth who were staring at her, their blue-haired heads brought close together for conspiratorial whispers. When they saw her looking back at them, they straightened and each looked in a different direction. She was getting more or less the same treatment from the pair of teenagers sitting on chrome stools a little ways down the counter from her.

She wondered if this was the treatment afforded all strangers in town or if her reputation, courtesy of Sheriff Harvey Gulch, had preceded her. Word traveled fast in small towns, and word of potential trouble the fastest of all. She'd hoped her luck would change after the morning she'd had. Tom's family doctor had examined her, questioned her, and reviewed her test results, but was unable to give her any hope. He said he couldn't tell her when, or if, her memory would return. He had been unable to suggest anything that would help heal her mind.

She'd agreed to meet Tom and Jamey here after her doctor's appointment. They had spent the morning shopping for groceries and other supplies. Impatiently she looked at her bare wrist, then made a fist with her hand and brought it down on the counter in frustration, causing the two teenagers to jump and look at her with renewed suspicion. She remembered that she used to have a wristwatch. Why the hell couldn't she remember who she was?

"What's a princess like you doing in a place like this?" Tom sat down on the stool on her left and Jamey climbed up onto the one on her right. She ruffled the boy's unruly hair and he smiled.

"Getting the evil eye from the townsfolk, mostly." Dorothy jerked her head in the direction of the women in the booth, who were staring again.

Tom put his cap on the empty stool next to him and ran a hand through this thick, onyx-colored hair. "Don't mind them. What do you want for lunch? Have you perused the extensive menu?" Tom gestured toward a blackboard with a few sandwiches listed on the far wall.

"Whatever you're having is fine."

"Clyde, we'll each have a burger with onion rings." Tom addressed the old soda jerk, who nodded and shuffled off toward the grill.

Jamey looked longingly at an ancient video game machine in the back of the store. "Dad, can I play Pac-Man until the burgers are done?"

"Sure." Tom reached into the pocket of his jeans and handed Jamey a couple of quarters. Jamey headed to the machine at a dead run.

Even though Tom seemed genuinely unconcerned about the stares of the others, Dorothy was still disturbed. He was reared in this town and was rearing his son here. These people were his friends and neighbors, and surely their good opinion meant something to him. She didn't want to be the source of any ugly gossip that might hurt Tom or Jamey. She'd take the sheriff up on his offer to stay in jail before she would do that.

"Tom," she began, not knowing exactly how to broach the subject. "If my staying at the farm gets to be a problem for you or Jamey, please don't hesitate to tell me and I'll find another place to live."

Tom's dark brows lifted in surprise. "You're not letting those old biddies and their nasty looks get to you, are you? It's probably true they don't approve of a young single woman staying with me and Jamey, but let me assure you, their talk doesn't bother me."

Dorothy had to smile a little. Tom was still protecting her from the sheriff's theory about her being a criminal. He knew full well that was the nature of the gossip about her, but he chose to put a less disturbing face on it for her sake. His thoughtfulness made her even more determined. "Listen, I'm sure you don't want to be the subject of ugly gossip in your own home town because of a woman."

Tom stared straight ahead and took a drink of the coffee that old Clyde had set before him. "It wouldn't be the first time."

The cryptic comment stopped her cold. She stared at his impassive face and wondered if he was going to elaborate, or if she could muster the nerve to ask him to.

"Fancy meeting you two here."

Tom and Dorothy tried to turn to see their visitor, but they swiveled their stools toward each other and bumped knees. Casey laughed and sat on the stool Jamey had just vacated. "Hope I didn't interrupt anything."

"We were just about to sample some of Clyde's four-star cuisine. Would you care to join us?"

"Can't, but thanks anyway. I'm just here to pick up my prenatal vitamins." She glanced towards Jamey, who was engrossed in the game.

Casey propped one elbow on the counter and looked at Dorothy. "So, how have you been? Any more explosions? Floods? Famines? Earthquakes?"

Dorothy laughed. "No, thank goodness." She was glad she and Jamey had decided to keep the dishwasher incident to themselves.

"Glad to hear it. By the way, the corn festival is coming up and it's going to be lots of fun. I really want you to come. You'll love it."

Tom made a snorting noise, eliciting a cold look from his sister, who turned her full attention to Dorothy. "There's going to be crafts and contests and exhibits, kind of like the fair we have in the fall. I'm president of the women's auxiliary that puts on this shindig, so you've both got to promise me here and now that you'll come."

Dorothy looked to Tom, who shrugged. "Sure," she said. "We'd love to."

"Oh, good!" Casey enthused. "The main event is the barn dance and this year it's a costume ball, so be thinking about what you're going to come as."

"I'm coming as a farmer," Tom said.

"How imaginative." Casey reached around Dorothy to punch him in the ribs. "My brother is nothing if not a good sport. I've really got to run now, so I'll see you at the festival if not before."

Dorothy watched Casey breeze out. She had a renewed sense of affection for Tom's sister. Casey had to have heard the gossip too. And she still was willing to give Dorothy the benefit of the doubt. Her visit to the farm the other day probably had much more to do with checking out her brother's new boarder than with delivering a stack of yearbooks. Dorothy was glad she had passed muster.

She turned to Tom. "Are you sure you don't mind going to the festival? I mean, if you'd rather I kept a low profile, I'd understand."

"Absolutely not. Now I don't want you to worry about that gossip. All these people really know about you is that you've lost your memory and Jamey calls you Dorothy because you got caught in the tornado. If they want to make up anything else, let 'em." Tom saw Clyde coming with their food and raised his voice. "We know the truth. You're Princess Dorothy of the Netherlands."

Clyde's wing-like brows shot upwards as he set their

plates in front of them and then he ambled back to the grill. Tom leaned toward Dorothy and whispered, "Those eyebrows are like antennae. He's the biggest gossip in this town. Odds are that by the time we go to the festival, half the people there will think you really *are* royalty."

After lunch Dorothy waited on the sidewalk beside the feed-and-seed store while Tom loaded large burlap bags into the truck. She feigned interest in the neighboring shop window while admiring Tom out of the corner of her eye. He shouldered what looked like hundred-pound bags as if they were packed with marshmallows instead of grain. The cotton jersey of his black T-shirt strained to contain his bulging biceps and stretched tight across his massive chest. At one point Tom caught her looking and broke into a devilish grin. She jerked her gaze back to the shop window and saw something that genuinely interested her.

The fabric store's window display consisted of colorful silks, but back farther into the shop itself Dorothy caught sight of a bolt of blue-and-white gingham. It looked like the same material as that of Judy Garland's pinafore in *The Wizard of Oz*. She put both hands up to shield her eyes from the sun so she could see better.

What was it Tom had said a while ago in the drugstore? All the townspeople knew about her was that she had no memory and Jamey had named her Dorothy for the girl in the movie. What better way to disarm these people than to prove she was a good sport? If she demonstrated that she could laugh at herself and her situation, perhaps they might warm to her a bit. In addition, it would be a big kick for Jamey, and maybe even for Tom as well.

Dorothy entered the shop and smiled cheerily at the clerk, who gave her a polite nod and a not-too-subtle once-over. She looked around and noticed a counter full of thick books, pattern books she supposed. Picking out a pattern must be the first step, she reasoned. So she looked through one of the books until she'd located a suitable jumper pattern and wrote down the number. She started to close the book when she noticed that it had a tab labeled "Costumes." To her delight, she found a section of animal costumes for children, one of which was a lion. She would make Jamey a Cowardly Lion outfit. Perfect!

The clerk, a middle-aged woman with tall red hair and even redder lipstick, shuffled over and located the patterns in a huge metal cabinet. She handed them to Dorothy.

Dorothy turned the patterns over and looked at the columns of figures, measurements in both centimeters and inches, on the back. She squinted at the tiny print. The numbers meant nothing to her. She would obviously have to contract the services of a seamstress. "Um, how do I go about finding someone to make these for me?"

"There are a couple of local seamstresses we give referrals to." The woman opened a drawer behind the counter and shuffled through a sheaf of papers. "Here's a price list."

"Hmm. Looks reasonable to me," Dorothy said, opening the small purse she'd bought earlier at a second-hand store. She reached instinctively for her gold card, and instead her hand closed around the folded bills Tom had given her. She fanned the money out some, hoping it was more than she thought it was. "Uh-oh."

Tom had visited the bank that morning so he could pay her wages in cash in case she saw something in town she wanted to buy. She took the money out and as she counted it, her spirits fell. She guessed she would have barely enough for the material, thread and patterns, with none left over for a seamstress. Then she remembered the old sewing machine in the corner of her bedroom. Could she possibly make the outfits herself? She looked at the front of the patterns again. The word "Simplicity" was emblazoned across the top in big, friendly letters. How hard could it be?

"I'm running a little low on cash, so I guess I'll have to make them myself."

The woman smiled benignly and raised one painted-on brow. "Do much sewing, do you?"

"No, actually. I'm a beginner. Can you help me get together all the things I'll need?"

"Sure. For starters, I'd recommend one of these." She held up a vicious-looking little tool that resembled a scalpel with a U-shaped blade."

Dorothy took a step backwards. "What's that?"

One corner of the woman's painted mouth quirked upwards, as did one brow, giving her face a lopsided look. "It's called a seam ripper. It's used for fixing mistakes. Not that you're going to make any."

"I'm telling you, Luther. We've got to pull another job, and soon. We're running out of dough." The man regarded his scruffy companion and noted, not for the first time, how the little man's eyes darted back and forth whenever they were out in public. "And for God's sake, quit looking so shifty-eyed. A cop could make you for a crook from a mile off."

Luther grimaced as they continued down the sidewalk and adjusted the folded bandanna he wore as a head-band. "Otis, don't be an idiot. We'll have more than just my shifty eyes to worry about unless we keep laying low. There's probably all kinds of bulletins out for us. Our pictures are probably in the post office, for cryin' out loud, and they ain't on the stamps. You know when that rich bitch got away from us, she had to have gone straight to the cops." He backhanded Otis across the chest for emphasis.

The tall, skinny man doubled over but kept walking. "Oh, yeah?" he replied, rubbing his chest. "Then how come we haven't seen anything about it on the news?"

Luther scratched his head. It was a good question and one they'd both been puzzling over since the Spencer woman had taken off. The kidnapping for ransom and subsequent escape of an heiress should have been front-page headlines in newspapers all over the country. Police artist sketches of Otis and him should have been on the eleven o'clock news. But they weren't.

In fact, their lack of exposure would have hurt his feelings if it had not also kept him out of jail. As he pondered this turn of events, he ran headlong into a man loading feed bags into a truckbed.

"Why the hell don't you watch what you're doing?" Luther exploded.

The man loading the truck straightened up to his full height and turned to face Luther. "Sorry."

Luther shrank back involuntarily as the man's chest filled his entire line of vision, blocking out the sun and everything else for that matter. His bravado faded under the muscleman's cool, green-eyed stare. "Yeah, well, just watch it next time, that's all."

Luther quickened his pace to put distance between himself and the huge man. Otis had to run a few steps to catch up with him. "I don't know why we had to try a kidnapping anyway. We were doing all right just pulling the burglaries and a robbery here and there. Why'd we have to go pulling a job that could get us locked up 'til we're old and gray?"

Luther scoffed. "Your problem is you got no ambition, Otis. You never think big. You'll be a small-time crook all your life."

"I don't care if I'm a big-time crook or a small-time crook, just so long as I don't wind up in the pen and I don't starve to death. What I want to know is, what do we do now?" Otis asked with a scowl.

The small, wiry man stopped in his tracks and wheeled on his partner in crime. "I don't know, damn it. But I'll tell you this much. If I ever see that chick again, I'll make her wish she was never born."

Dorothy cut the costume pieces out of the cloth that night, and the next morning after breakfast she was ready to begin sewing. She'd told Tom that she was making herself a Sunday dress but hadn't shown him or Jamey the material. She'd start on Jamey's Cowardly

Lion costume first. She regretted that she couldn't keep his costume a surprise as hers would be, but she knew he would have to stand for a fitting before she was finished.

The patterns had been difficult enough to decipher, but threading the ancient sewing machine had been even worse. She had stuck herself more than once trying to get the needle into position to be threaded before she had discovered the round crank on the side of the machine. Her bad luck with machines had made her wary of this one, and she'd approached it with the stealth one would a sleeping Bengal tiger.

It must have been one of the first electric sewing machines ever made. The foot-operated power control was stiff and had a tendency to become stuck in high speed. The thick plush material she'd selected for the lion's coat was difficult to work with, so the sewing was awkward. Her confidence waned after the material refused to feed under the needle properly, but she kept going. She'd started this project, and she would finish it if it killed her.

Halfway into one of the side seams, with the material lurching beneath her fingers jerkily, the machine became stuck on high speed. She took her foot from the power button but it did no good. The machine was eating up material like a crazed B-movie robot. "Stop it! Give it back!" She tugged on the material for all she was worth, but the greedy thing wouldn't yield. She stood up and looked at the controls on top of the machine for some kind of switch that would put the thing in reverse. No luck. That was when she became aware that something was *really* wrong.

She looked down and saw that the tail of her chambray work shirt had become caught in the machine when she stood up. She felt herself being pulled chest-first toward the wildly pounding needle. Her mind flashed crazily on her earlier vow to finish the project if it killed her. Little did she know that it actually might do just that. She dove for the power cord and yanked it as hard as she could. The contraption clattered to a halt.

It took forever to free herself and the bunched-up mess from the jaws of the machine, and when she did, she realized why the lady at the store had insisted that she buy the seam ripper. It was going to come in handy.

She was oiling the foot control with some machine oil that she'd found when she heard the familiar slam of the screen door downstairs. "Dorothy, come quick!" she heard Jamey shout. "Look what we've got!"

Dorothy went to the window and looked out. A truck pulling a horse trailer was heading down the driveway toward the main road. In the corral was a handsome bay horse. She smiled as she ran out of the house to the corral. A new animal on the farm, particularly a horse, would get Jamey so excited he would be beside himself.

"Isn't she a beauty?" Jamey asked, stroking the horse's neck.

"She certainly is." The mare was a deep reddish brown with a white blaze that went from her soulful brown eyes to her velvety nose. She didn't flinch when Dorothy stroked her sleek neck, but took a step toward her and nuzzled her side gently. "What a friendly little thing she is."

"She likes you," Jamey said, beaming.

Dorothy was surprised and pleased. "I think you may be right."

"I like a horse with good taste." Tom stood next to her with a saddle over his shoulder. With his free hand, he plucked a piece of string from her hair and pointed to the front of her shirt. "What's that?"

She looked down. A fringe of thread trailed off from the jagged seam running zig-zag down one side of her shirt where she'd had to cut it free from the material of the costume. She met his gaze with a straight face. "It's just a little wearable art project I've been working on upstairs. So, where'd you get the horse?"

With one last, skeptical glance at her shirt, he said, "When the vet was here last, he told us about some folks who needed to board their horse long-term. I'll use the money to buy Jamey a horse of his own, since Silvester is getting up in age and really can't be ridden anymore. Until then, Jamey can ride Emily here all he wants."

She continued to stroke the mare's neck as Tom arranged the tack. Perhaps it was silly, but she believed the horse *did* like her. She thought she remembered someone once telling her that you either had a way with horses or you didn't. Looking into the animal's affectionate, dark eyes, she felt that she must be someone who had an affinity for horses.

As Tom saddled the horse, he reviewed each step of the process with Jamey. By the time he got to the part about fastening the girth properly, Dorothy was convinced that she herself had saddled a horse before, many times in fact. Her spirits soared. This was the first time since seeing the picture in the yearbook that she recognized something familiar. She knew about horses.

Tom helped Jamey mount the mare and led them around the corral, apparently to satisfy himself that the horse was as gentle as she seemed. Dorothy watched them go around and around, the monotonous sight lulling her into a state of utter relaxation. The morning sun was pleasantly warm on her skin, adding to her sense of serenity. Then something inexplicable happened.

A different image intruded into her consciousness, a scene remarkably similar to the one she was actually witnessing, only the people and perspective were different. Instead of Jamey, *she* was the child on the horse. And instead of Tom leading the horse, there was a tall, lanky man, who looked back at her with a wink and a smile.

The image flashed into her mind for a split second and then was gone, the way a bolt of lightning illuminates the darkness for only an instant. She blinked once, twice. Jamey and Tom were back beside her. The only impression the phantom image had left behind was a vague feeling of affection for the man she had seen.

Who was the man teaching her to ride? He had looked at her with such warm, paternal devotion. Was he her father? Her pulse quickened with excitement and her eyes grew moist. Her father! That's why she had flashed on the image as she watched Tom and Jamey. Her subconscious mind had remembered back to when her own father had taught her to ride a horse. That had to be the explanation.

She stifled the urge to call out to Tom, to share what had just happened, but instead she decided to keep the experience to herself for a little while and savor the moment, so long in coming, that she actually remembered something significant about her past.

After a few moments, Tom gave the boy a few additional instructions, handed him the reins, and walked back to the center of the corral where Dorothy stood.

"She's perfect for him," she observed.

"Yes, I think so too." Tom turned his gaze from the boy and the horse to her. "Speaking of being perfect for him, I've been meaning to tell you . . ." He paused, searching for the right words. "You've been great for Jamey. He's a lot happier than he was before you came to stay with us." He looked down and rearranged some dirt with his boot. When he looked up, his eyes were full of warmth and gratitude. "I guess what I'm saying is . . . thanks."

Dorothy felt herself glow with happiness. First her amazing vision, then Tom's few simple words of praise, had made her feel better than she had in as far back as she could remember. "I should be thanking you. You've opened your home to me, trusted me with your son. I'll never be able to thank you enough. If it weren't for you, I'd be mopping floors at the jail right now."

As she looked at Tom, she felt once again the undeniable pull of attraction to him and saw it reflected back to her in his eyes. Those beautiful eyes, sea green in the bright sunlight. Mutual need—magnetic, electric, powerful—crackled between them. She felt herself moving toward him, and he took a step toward her.

"Whoa!"

Startled, she at first took Jamey's shout as a call for restraint to Tom and her, not as a command to the horse.

THE PUBLISHERS OF ZEBRA BOUQUET

are making this special offer to lovers of contemporary romances to introduce this exciting new line of novels. Zebra Bouquet Romances have been praised by critics and authors alike as being of the highest quality and best written romantic fiction available today.

EACH FULL-LENGTH NOVEL

has been written by authors you know and love as well as by up-and-coming writers that you'll only find with Zebra Bouquet. We'll bring you the newest novels by world famous authors like Vanessa Grant, Judy Gill Ann Josephson and award winning Suzanne Barrett and Leigh Greenwood—to name just a few. Zebra Bouquet's editors have selected only the very best and highest quality romances for up-and-coming publications under the Bouquet banner.

YOU'LL BE TREATED

to tales of star-crossed lovers in glamourous settings that are sure to captivate you. These stories will keep you enthralled to the very happy end.

4 FREE NOVELS As a way to introduce you to these terrific romances, the publishers of Bouquet are offering Zebra Romance readers Four Free Bouquet novels. They are yours for the asking with no obligation to buy a single book. Read them at your leisure. We are sure that after you've read these introductory books you'll want more! (If you do not wish to receive any further Bouquet novels, simply write "cancel" on the invoice and return to us within 10 days.)

SAVE 20% WITH HOME DELIVERY Each month you'll receive four just-published Bouquet romances. We'll ship them to you as soon as they are printed (you may even get them before the bookstores). You'll have 10 days to preview these exciting novels for Free. If you decide to keep them, you'll be billed the special preferred home subscription price of just $3.20 per book; a total of just $12.80 — that's a savings of 20% off the publisher's price. If for any reason you are not satisfied simply return the novels for full credit, no questions asked. You'll never have to purchase a minimum number of books and you may cancel your subscription at any time.

GET STARTED TODAY –
NO RISK AND NO OBLIGATION

To get your introductory gift of 4 Free Bouquet Romances fill out and mail the
enclosed Free Book Certificate today. We'll ship your free books as soon as we
receive this information. Remember that you are under no obligation. This is
a risk-free offer from the publishers of Zebra Bouquet Romances.

Call us TOLL FREE at 1-888-345-BOOK
Visit our website at www.kensingtonbooks.com

FREE BOOK CERTIFICATE

YES! I would like to take you up on your offer. Please send me 4 Free Bouquet Romance Novels as my introductory gift. I understand that unless I tell you otherwise, I will then receive the 4 newest Bouquet novels to preview each month FREE for 10 days. If I decide to keep them I'll pay the preferred home subscriber's price of just $3.20 each (a total of only $12.80) plus $1.50 for shipping and handling. That's a 20% savings off the publisher's price. I understand that I may return any shipment for full credit–no questions asked–and I may cancel this subscription at any time with no obligation. Regardless of what I decide to do, the 4 Free Introductory Novels are mine to keep as Bouquet's gift.

BN080A

Name _____

Address _____

City _____ State _____ Zip _____

Telephone ( ) _____

Signature _____

(If under 18, parent or guardian must sign.)

Orders subject to acceptance by Zebra Home Subscription Service. Terms and Prices subject to change.
Order valid only in the U.S.

If this response card is missing,
call us at 1-888-345-BOOK.

Be sure to visit our website at
www.kensingtonbooks.com

BOUQUET ROMANCES
Zebra Home Subscription Service, Inc.
P.O. Box 5214
Clifton NJ 07015-5214

PLACE
STAMP
HERE

She and Tom both laughed nervously and backed away from each other a step or two.

"What's wrong, sport? Are you tired of riding already?" Tom asked.

"No. I just wanted Dorothy to have a turn."

Tom turned to her again. "Would you like to take a spin?"

"Sure."

Tom stepped forward to readjust the stirrup straps, but Dorothy reached them first and did it herself. She knew, from somewhere far away, just how to do it, how much room she needed to adjust them to her height. She had a vague idea that she was more used to riding with an English saddle than a Western one, but she still knew what to do. When she was done, she put her foot in the stirrup and swung herself into the saddle as if she'd done it all her life.

Dorothy nudged the mare with her heels and the little horse responded. She rode around the corral slowly at first and soon felt herself get into the rhythm of riding. As she urged the horse to a trot, her hips found that back-and-forth posting motion that she knew she'd once been taught. Instinctively, she put the horse through her paces until they settled on an easy gallop. The horse responded to her every command, no matter how subtle.

Riding felt as natural to her as anything she could remember doing. She closed her eyes for a moment and turned her face to the sun. It was as if she were flying. Pure joy radiated through her, from her brief memory of her past, because of what Tom had said, and from the ride itself.

Tom was right. She did have a definite rapport with

Jamey. And because of that, she was developing a growing sense of belonging, of being useful, of making a difference in the lives of others. Dishwashers and vacuum cleaners be damned. Tom had said she was "great" with Jamey, and that was the most important thing of all.

She felt more alive than she could ever remember feeling. And she was sure that even if she could remember her old life, she would be able to recall no more perfect moment. She reined the horse to a stop in front of Tom and Jamey. Tom stood rigid, his arms crossed, an odd expression on his face. He almost looked displeased.

She dismounted and Jamey came toward her. "Wow! You really know how to ride," he said. He allowed her to help him back onto the horse and started off again.

Dorothy strode purposefully toward Tom, and by the time she reached him, he'd rearranged his features into a benign expression.

"Jamey's right. You *do* know how to ride."

Some of her hair had come loose from the elastic band that held it. She gathered it up again and secured it with a snap of the band. She had a feeling he would tell her what was bothering him soon enough. "Looks like it."

Tom rocked back on his heels and watched Jamey across the corral. "Actually, the way you handled that horse, I think it's more accurate to say you look like a top-notch competitive rider."

Dorothy put her hands on her hips. She was annoyed that his strange reaction had ruined her exuberant mood.

"The way you were looking at me just now—it wasn't admiration for my riding skills I saw on your face."

He glanced toward her briefly and continued, his voice taking on a forced casualness. "I think we have another clue to your background. My guess is that you've had some schooling in the equestrian arts."

She frowned, not liking where this line of reasoning could lead. "You mean, like professional instruction?"

"Yes. Exactly. You're that good." Tom managed a smile but she could see that it was forced.

Could it be? Was the man in the image just a hired riding teacher and not her father at all? Her spirits dropped as she realized the vision might have been as insignificant as a passing daydream. Just for a moment, she'd had a father, if only in her mind. Then Tom's remarks had taken him away from her. And on top of that, Tom's conjecture had given him another perfect excuse to stereotype her.

"So I guess this is just further evidence that I'm a rich, spoiled city girl and not cut out to live on the farm." Her eyes issued a challenge.

"I didn't say any of that. But I do think it's important that we both be realistic. This isn't your world, and it's only a matter of time until you become dissatisfied." He said it with the same cold air of detachment that made her want to scream.

"Don't tell me how to feel." He said nothing. She wanted to rail about his unfairness, his prejudice, and his pigheadedness, but she knew it would do no good. He was in ice man mode.

She managed a parting wave and smile for Jamey, then went back into the house and up to her room. Resuming her sewing, she found herself fidgety and unable to concentrate. Finally, she laid her head on her crossed arms. So much for her earlier warm, fuzzy feelings of belonging.

Feeling suddenly confined, she wanted to get out of the little room and back out into the sunshine, but she wanted no more to do with Tom until she had to face him at suppertime. Looking out her window in the direction of the north pasture, she got an idea. If she was careful, she would be able to reach her destination without being seen by Tom. She went downstairs, got the basket she'd used for the picnic, and slipped out of the house.

After a few minutes' walk, she opened the gate to what Tom called the north pasture and headed for the spot where they'd had their picnic. She would gather some apples from the tree and try her hand at making that apple pie Jamey wanted. She laughed to herself. How much more like a good Midwestern farm wife could she get than baking an apple pie? She paused, basket in hand. Wife? Where had that come from? She shook her head. She wondered how different her present domestic role was from her own life. Pretty darned far, she guessed, because that's exactly what it felt like—a role to be played.

She just couldn't get the hang of domestic engineering, as Tom liked to call it. It wasn't that she didn't care about doing a good job. She adored Jamey and wanted to please Tom for all the kindness he'd shown her. It was just that nothing came easily or naturally to her. She sighed. Maybe Tom was right after all. She didn't belong here.

Wading through the tall grass, she thought guiltily about Tom and their earlier conversation. Since he hadn't known about the vision she'd had, he hadn't realized that he had hurt her feelings. Her attitude must have seemed like an overreaction to him. Maybe she should apologize.

She reached the tree and stood on tiptoe to pluck one of the apples. It was not yet ripe and neither, it appeared, were any of the others. She'd failed to notice that the other day. Oh well, she thought, she'd just put more sugar in the pie and cook it longer to soften the fruit. She reached for another apple, and as her hand touched the rough, green skin, she heard a noise like a blast furnace belching fire. She knew that sound, and she'd never forget it if she lived to be a hundred.

Oh, no.

She froze, knowing instinctively not to make any sudden moves. Not that she could have moved anyway with the blood having crystallized in her veins. She turned her head as slowly as she could, just far enough to look behind her. It was Hickory, all right. And it didn't look as if his recent amorous activities had mellowed him out any. He eyed her with bloodshot malice and stamped one foot like an impudent child calling for attention.

"You've got it, you hairy sonofabitch. You've got my full attention," she said under her breath. "Now, take this!" She wheeled, and with rapid-fire movements, ripped the apple from its stem and hurled it and the basket at the beast. In the next second, she rushed toward the tree, planted her foot as high on the trunk as she could, and thrust herself upward toward the highest branch she could reach.

By the time the enormous bull recovered from the shock of the assault and got itself moving, her momentum had enabled her to swing up onto the branch. By the time he was fully into his charge, she had gone on to the next higher branch, which put her out of his reach. He stopped as he pulled even with her, his bovine brain apparently grasping the futility of head butting a tree.

Dorothy wedged herself tightly against the trunk and tried to catch her breath. She could have sworn she heard Tom say that the bull was not usually kept in this pasture. Tom's neighbors must've left a gate open somewhere when they returned him the other day. The monster gazed sullenly up at her, threw back its head and bellowed.

"Oh, yeah? Well, get this—if it was up to me, you'd find yourself swimming upstream in special sauce between two sesame seed buns. How do you like that, you ugly hamburger on the hoof?"

The bull snorted and glared. Dorothy settled back against the tree and tried to get comfortable, which wasn't easy, as gnarled and rough as the tree was. She plucked another apple and tasted it. It was so bitter she had to spit it out, directing her aim at Hickory. He caught the bite of apple between his horns. He went cross-eyed for a moment, trying to see what had hit him.

"Bull's eye!" Dorothy shouted. "If you'll pardon the expression." Hickory only looked angrier. This bull had no sense of humor whatsoever.

Dorothy looked around her and shivered despite the warmth of the morning. Tree branches with their clusters of leaves hung all around her face. A tiny yellow inchworm worked its way awkwardly across a twig four inches from her nose. She wondered what other creepy, crawly things lived on the leaves and involuntarily scratched her arms. Had she ever climbed a tree before? She doubted it. Escaping danger was the only good reason she could think of for anyone to do such a thing. She'd heard of children doing it for fun, but she couldn't imagine what was fun about it. The inchworm fell off the leaf and landed squarely on the end of her sneaker. She shuddered and shook it off.

She looked back down at the bull, who was still staring at her menacingly but with unnerving calm. From time to time, she could hear the hiss of his breath or a swish of his tail as he flicked a fly off his flank. He obviously had all day to wait for her to come down. It was a real Mexican standoff, if ever there was one. Where were those roaming bands of Indians when you needed them?

Eight

Tom mounted the stairs, pausing only to glance at Jamey, who was sitting in front of the TV, absorbed in a cartoon program. It was almost noon, and Dorothy was not in the kitchen preparing lunch as she usually was at this hour.

He knew he had annoyed her earlier with his speculation about her background, but she didn't seem like the type who would hole up in her room and pout when she felt slighted. That had been more Margaret's style. Maybe she was just working on another of those weird wearable art projects, although he hadn't heard the sewing machine. When he reached her door, he knocked on it tentatively, but received no answer.

"Dorothy," he called softly. Still no answer. He turned the knob and opened the door.

The room looked like it had been the site of the famous fight between the gingham dog and the calico cat. Bits of thread and shredded material lay all over the sewing machine, floor, and bed. But there was no Dorothy.

Curious, he walked closer to the machine and examined the bulky wad of brown plush cloth. If she was making a Sunday dress, she'd picked some really weird material to do it with. Then he picked up one of the patterns that lay on the bed. It had a photograph of a child in a lion suit. Of course. She was making Jamey a costume for the masquerade party at the corn festival.

Tom sat on the bed beside a little pile of notions— thread, a couple of zippers, some snaps. He picked up a book called *Sewing Made Easy.* She obviously didn't know the first thing about sewing, but she'd gamely tried her best, just as she had done with all her household chores. And though some of those chores had literally backfired on her, still she kept her determination and good humor.

And had he encouraged her? No. His words of praise had been few and far between. As a reward for all her earnest efforts, he gave her lectures about how she wasn't fit for life on the farm because she was probably from the city and probably rich and spoiled. Tom hung his head and squeezed his eyes shut for a moment.

When he opened them, his gaze fell on a slip of paper sticking out from the pages of the sewing book. It was the cash register receipt for the material. He looked at it and winced. The amount of money he'd been able to give her for her wages was pitifully small. Out of all the things she must have wanted and needed, she'd spent most if not all of her money on a gift for his son.

He felt a renewed pang of guilt for their unpleasant exchange earlier that morning. She'd been so happy when she was riding. He saw it on her face. But when she reined the horse a stop and saw his look of disapproval, her joy fell away. And now she was missing. He wouldn't have blamed her if she'd just taken off, but she had no place to go. Where could she be?

Dorothy soon tired of standing crouched against the tree trunk with bug-infested leaves tickling her face. She discovered that if she sat down on the branch she'd been standing on, her feet dangled just out of Hickory's reach. This seemed to annoy the bull even more, which pleased her.

The position of the sun told her it was noon, or there-abouts. Surely Tom would miss her soon. The bull still stared at her malevolently. From time to time, he stretched his neck upward to sniff her tennis shoes with his wet, pinkish-gray nose.

"Yeesh." She kicked at him, but he barely flinched.

Just as she had begun to contemplate what it would be like to spend the night in an apple tree dangling precariously over a half-ton of mean-tempered bull, she heard the faint, faraway sound of a tractor motor. Hickory heard it too, and looked around. Dorothy heaved a sigh of relief as Tom came into view, driving the tractor and waving. The bull looked from the tractor to Dorothy, as if trying to make up his sluggish mind. When Tom was almost to the tree, some of the other cows began to bellow far away. Access to the cows seemed to be the deciding factor for Hickory. He loped off in the direction of the racket.

Tom stopped the tractor a few yards from the tree and jumped down from the cab. "How's it going?"

Dorothy swung her feet back and forth. "Oh, can't complain."

He put his thumbs through the belt loops of his jeans and grinned up at her. "I'm sorry this happened. Hickory isn't supposed to be in this pasture. The neighbors who borrowed him took him through the wrong gate when they brought him back. I just dumped some hay back there at the entrance to the other pasture, the one where the cows are. Between the hay and the cows, he'll be too distracted to come back this way anytime soon."

"Hmm." It sounded like a reasonable explanation. "Where's Jamey, anyway?"

"I gave him a bunch of chores to do. He'll be busy for quite a while." He picked up the basket. "Looks like you were going to try to make that pie anyway, huh?"

"That's right. Did you think that just because you said it would be difficult, that I wouldn't try?" She made no move to jump down, but continued to swing her legs as if she were relaxing on the porch swing rather than stuck up a tree. She decided she liked this perspective on things. Usually, she had to look up at *him*.

Tom squinted into the sun as he looked up at her, giving his eyes a catlike quality. He tossed the basket aside. "Not at all. In fact, I was just now thinking about how I admire your willingness to take on difficult jobs."

"I'll just bet you were."

"Seriously. I went up to your room to look for you, and I saw how your sewing project was going."

Dorothy felt herself color with embarrassment. "Oh, now I see where you're going with this. You're going to give me a hard time about my sewing ability." She sniffed and looked at something in the distance. "Or lack thereof."

"Not at all."

His expression became a bit more serious, and she thought she read real admiration in it. Imagine that. She couldn't help thinking how fabulous his eyes, with their thick fringe of coal-black lashes, looked from this angle. He hadn't shaved that morning, and a beard as black as his hair had begun to shadow his face. Through the loose-fitting neck of his cotton shirt, she could also see the outline of his pectoral muscles with their mat of crisp, springy, black hair. Her mouth watered slightly, and it wasn't from the sour apple she just tasted.

Tom shifted his weight and looked away for a moment. "I think it was incredibly generous of you to spend most of your money on Jamey's costume. Not to mention the time and energy you're putting into making it yourself." He looked back up at her and smiled the most beautiful smile she'd ever seen. "And I'm sure that with your determination and positive attitude, it will be a great success."

"Thank you." Despite the interesting view, Dorothy was suddenly struck by the urge to be on the ground beside him. "Would you help me down?"

"I thought you'd never ask."

He stepped closer and reached both arms up to her. She leaned down and put her hands on his forearms. As she slid off the branch, he lifted her gently into his powerful arms and let her settle against his chest. Her arms slid naturally along his until they came to rest on his shoulders. Her cheek lay against his chest, and she could hear his heart beating like a trip-hammer. Or was

it her own? Her senses seemed confused, overwhelmed.
She thought her feet were now touching the ground, but
she wasn't sure. Was that really his mouth brushing the
top of her head with a kiss? A throbbing warmth spread
throughout her body.

Instead of letting her go, he tightened his arms around
her, and she reveled in the hard, lean contours of his
body and his clean male scent. His hands moved in lazy
circles on her back. "I didn't mean to hurt your feelings
earlier," he whispered hoarsely in her ear. "I never want
to hurt you, but I'm not real tactful, see? Sometimes
the things I want to say don't come out exactly right."

"Mmm hmm," she agreed. As he pressed a soft,
sweet kiss to her neck, a jolt went through her and her
knees buckled. He was now supporting all her weight,
but he seemed not to notice.

He raised his head, and for a moment she was afraid
he would let her go, but instead he ran his hand along
her cheek and cupped her chin. His work-roughened
skin sent a tickling sensation all along her spine in a
delicious shiver. He tipped her head up and brought his
face close to hers. His eyes were smoky with need, but
troubled as well. "Please believe I never want to hurt
you."

After a moment she found her voice. "Of course I
believe you."

His expression reflected the warring emotions of sorrow and desire. He lifted her still limp body and crushed
her against him, bringing his lips down on hers posses-
sively, insistently. Her arms went around his neck and
she clung to him, feeling the incredible strength of his
steel-like body and the power of his emotions.

He slanted his mouth against hers, teasing her tongue with his own. She didn't realize he was lowering her to the ground until she felt the spongy earth against her shoulder. He slipped one of his hands under her to cup her bottom, causing her to arch her back against him. His lips began a descent down her neck, nipping and licking. She could hear his breath coming in rasping gulps.

His hands were working themselves under her T-shirt now, searing her body as they went up and up. He took his lips from her collarbone just long enough to lift her shirt up and off. Her fingers trembled as she began unfastening his shirt buttons. He shrugged out of his shirt and pressed his face to her cleavage while she ran her hands along every rigid muscle of his back and shoulders.

"So soft. So sweet," he muttered. She gasped for breath as his raspy cheeks and chin, with their day's growth of beard, etched her skin. His hand came to the side of her breast, squeezing gently, massaging. His tongue slipped underneath the edge of the lace. Her entire body throbbed with passion, and she twined her fingers through his hair.

His hands came to the front closure of her bra, but his large fingers fumbled with the tiny hooks. She took her hands from his hair and began to unfasten them herself, and he pressed kisses on the backs of her fingers, running his tongue along each one. She'd undone two hooks when she realized that he'd frozen in place. She looked up at him to see that he was staring blankly at her hands, blinking like a man who'd just been hit over the head with a plank.

She stopped unhooking the bra. "What is it?"

He sat up shakily and took her left hand in his. Gently, he stroked the place where the ring had been. They'd both forgotten the damned ring. The spot where it had been was almost undetectable now. There was no indentation and the band of white skin was only slightly paler than the rest of her hand. But they both knew what the mark had looked like only a couple of weeks ago. And they both knew what it meant.

"We can't." He released her hand and jammed his own through his disheveled hair. "What if we make love and your husband shows up next week? Or worse than that, what if he shows up next month? By that time, we'd both be in so deep. . . ." He looked up at her, his eyes bright with alarm. "It would be a nightmare."

Aching from losing the feel of his body on hers, she opened her mouth to protest, but words didn't come. How did she know that if she made love with Tom, she wouldn't be cheating on a loving husband? What *would* she do if she became involved with him and a man she'd sworn to share her life with came along to claim her? She put her hands to her temples as her head began to pound. "But I don't *feel* married," she said weakly. "Just like I don't feel like I'm a mother."

Tom reached for his shirt and began to put it on. "It's not just that. It's your whole life."

"What do you mean?" Dorothy had refastened her bra and was putting on her own shirt.

Tom let out a long breath as he buttoned his shirt. "I know I've given you a hard time about being a rich city girl. But think about it. You might have a fabulous life somewhere. A life that you'd jump at the chance to go back to if you only knew it existed."

She wanted to tell him that she didn't care what other life she might have, she only wanted to be there for him and Jamey. Then she remembered what had led her to seek the solitude of this meadow to begin with—her frustration with the life she was leading. The way it was foreign to her, unnatural to her. She felt him smoothing her hair and looked up at him, standing over her.

"You're right," she said finally. "It's got to be hands-off for you and me from now on."

He gave her a forced smile and extended his hand. She allowed him to pull her to her feet, and then they stood there, hand in hand, for a long moment. Finally, Tom said, "I know that we haven't had a chance to do much serious work toward finding out who you are. I know you've made some calls and had someone search the Internet. But other than that, we've just been waiting for your memory to come back on its own, and it looks like that might not be enough. Planting will be over in a week or so—about the time of the corn festival. After that, I won't have to be in the field as much for a while."

He took her other hand in his and gave them both a gentle, reassuring squeeze. "I promise you that after the festival, we'll do whatever we have to in order to find out your identity. We'll go look around the university where you thought you saw something familiar, take ads out in all the papers, or whatever it takes."

She managed a nod and a smile, even though her body was still tingling with the loss of what his body and his lips had promised a few minutes earlier. "Thanks."

"Good. Now, we've got a real plan for finding out who you are." Tom released her hands and gestured toward the tractor. "Hey, ever ridden one of those before?"

She shook her head and laughed. He spoke as if he were offering her a ride in a chauffeured stretch limousine. It had to be a *guy* thing. "I can't say that I have."

"Well you're in for a treat. But first let's pick some apples for that pie."

Although she and Tom tried their best to be nonchalant and jovial at lunch and dinner, Dorothy could tell that Jamey sensed something was amiss. He was subdued all day. She, on the other hand, was a bundle of frustrated, misdirected energy. All she could think of was Tom, his kiss, the feel of his body on hers. She was leery of returning to the sewing machine again in her present state of mind, since any loss of concentration could cost her her life, or her shirt at least. But she had to do something or she'd go crazy. And sewing had the added benefit of being an excellent way to avoid being in the same room with Tom.

By seven-thirty, she decided she was at the point where she needed Jamey to stand for a fitting, so she went to the head of the stairs and called him up. He came up the stairs listlessly, his head down, and followed her meekly to her room. He smiled for a moment when she showed him the photo of his costume on the pattern cover, but his sorrowful look returned a few seconds later.

"Jamey, what's wrong? I thought you'd be thrilled about your costume."

"I am."

Dorothy sat on the bed and reached out for him. "Then what's wrong?"

He allowed her to gather him to her and put her arm around his shoulders. "It's you and dad. I thought you liked him, and he liked you."

"We do." So that was it. It was the strained vibes he'd picked up on during lunch and dinner. He was a very perceptive little boy. "We did have a small difference of opinion this morning. But we, er, talked things out, and things between us are fine now."

Jamey brightened a little. He probably would have been able to tell if she'd been lying. But, for the most part, she was telling the truth.

"Honest?"

"Honest." She ruffled his hair and gave him a pat on the behind. "Now, let's see how this lion suit I've been working on is going to fit you."

Jamey obediently stepped into it, and it immediately swallowed him whole.

"Hmm. Maybe I should have measured you first." She gathered up a double handful of excess material at Jamey's midsection.

While she was trying to figure out what to do to fix the costume, Jamey said, "I'm glad you and Dad aren't mad at each other. Margaret was mad at him all the time."

Dorothy looked up. How strange that the little boy called his mommy by her first name. "She was? Why?"

Jamey shrugged. "Don't know. Seemed like she was sad all the time. Dad bought her presents and flowers, but it didn't make her any happier." He gave her a meaningful look. "They fought a lot."

"I'm sorry, Jamey. I know that must have been rough on you."

Jamey shrugged, then looked at her with his expressive headlamp eyes. "Dorothy, are you happy?"

She swallowed hard, thinking about how her day had gone and the conclusions she had reached—her feelings for Tom and her frustration at not being able to act on them. She knew that if she lied to him, he would sense it immediately. She picked up the fuzzy tail of the lion's costume and tickled his nose with it until he collapsed into her arms in a fit of giggles. "I am so happy to be your friend, that I could just roar!"

In the silence of the study, Tom could faintly hear his son's shrill laughter and what sounded like Dorothy doing a lion imitation. He threw his pencil onto the desk and propped his head in his hands. What the hell had he been thinking this afternoon? He'd almost made love to her right there in the grass.

He hadn't been able to get the encounter out of his mind all day, and his body still ached at the thought of it. He swore he could still taste her on his lips. And then he'd come to his senses, and all that was left was this terrible longing and the feel of her body branded into his. My God, he thought, and let his hands fall across the ledger on which he'd been working. What if they'd gone through with it? What if he'd let himself fall hopelessly in love with her and then, a month later, a man came to the door and said: Say, buddy, thanks for taking care of my wife. I've come to take her home with me now. Have a nice life.

He leaned back in the old-fashioned wooden desk chair and his gaze came to rest on a photo of Jamey. For God's sake, what about *him?* He was already so attached to the woman that he was going to be heart-broken when she left. Coupled with the pain of being abandoned by his mother still fresh in his mind, would the poor kid ever recover? Would *he?*

He couldn't, for the life of him, figure how he had been so stupid. How he could have let this happen? He closed his eyes, and then he knew. Her image—the way she'd looked there on the grass—came to life in his mind. Silky hair haloed her angel's face. Eyes as blue as the sky looked up at him, wanting him, needing him as much as he needed her.

He clutched his head and opened his eyes. No. He wouldn't do this. He would put her out of his mind, not just for the sake of him and Jamey, but for her sake as well. If she stayed much longer, he and his dreams would only wind up destroying her. Just like they had his marriage.

The next morning, Dorothy decided that baking the apple pie would be just the diversion she needed to for-get about what happened by the creek with Tom. She found a cookbook in the pantry and selected a suitable recipe. As she mixed the ingredients for the crust, she found that as a diversionary tactic, pie baking didn't cut it.

She couldn't get the things Tom had said to her, not to mention the feel of his body, out of her mind. And then there were Jamey's remarks, which had only confirmed her worst fears about Tom and Margaret's marriage. Her heart ached for Tom. Why had he said all that about hurting her? She felt that it was she who was hurting him, even though that was the last thing in the world that she wanted.

We'd both be in so deep, he'd said. No wonder he didn't want to get involved with anyone again, especially someone who was bound to up and leave him and his little boy at any time. She was a fool, an inconsiderate fool, to have ever let what almost happened almost happen.

She took her frustration out on the pastry dough, kneading it roughly until her fingers were tired. It became sticky so she sifted some flour onto the mess and started again. She stopped what she was doing and put down the sifter. How had she known to do that? It made sense, and she probably would have settled on that solution anyway had she thought about it long enough. But she did it instinctively. She grabbed the cookbook and scanned the recipe again. The instructions for preparing the pastry crust were sketchy. There were no tips on how to deal with sticky dough.

She looked down at her white apron and a flash of memory projected itself onto her consciousness. It was the image of a middle-aged woman, also in a white apron, smiling broadly at her, rolling out dough with a rolling pin. The woman sifted a dusting of flour onto the dough, and her image vanished. Dorothy was alone in the kitchen again, covered with sticky bits of dough and flour.

"Oh, my!" She leaned on the counter and took a deep breath. Who was that woman? She sensed that it was someone who had been close to her. She was left with a warm feeling of affection for the woman, just like with the man she'd imagined yesterday. She squeezed her eyes tightly shut and tried to remember exactly what the woman had looked like. She couldn't conjure up her face again, but she now remembered that she was wearing a uniform under the apron. The cook.

But that was okay, she told herself to stifle her disappointment. At least the memories were coming now, and quickly. That was the important thing. First the riding teacher, then the cook. It was a start. Of course, if the woman she saw was her family's cook, that was more evidence to support Tom's "rich girl" theory. Why could she remember the hired help but not her family? She sighed.

Now if she could only remember the man in her life, if there really was one. That made her think about Tom, and she became uneasy again. If she did remember a man in her life, would his touch be as tender as his body was powerful? Would his hair be as black and wavy? Would his eyes be as green as emeralds and as wily as a cat's when he smiled? He would have to be an exceptional man to measure up to Tom Weaver.

When she finished the crust, she began peeling apples, and soon spied a wormhole in one. "Ick!" She considered cutting out the bad place and salvaging the rest of the apple, but she was afraid she might come face to face with the worm. Or worse yet, half the worm. As she pondered what to do, she felt a poke in the small of her back.

"Put 'em up, partner! And drop that knife!"

"Oh, no! You've got me!" Dorothy cried helplessly. She heard Jamey giggle as she slowly turned to face him. "Don't shoot me, Mister, I'm just . . ." She looked down and saw him brandishing a toy revolver. ". . . the cook."

He had a red bandanna tied across his face in the manner of an Old West bandit. Only in an instant, he wasn't Jamey at all. And it wasn't a toy pistol. A new image superimposed itself over Jamey's and swam in her field of vision until she was dizzy. A charge of adrenaline shot though her, and she almost dropped the knife.

Jamey giggled at his little prank and went out the door, unaware that her shocked reaction had been real. She laid the knife on the counter and became aware that Tom had been watching the episode with Jamey from the dining room doorway.

He evidently could see that she was in distress about something because he was at her side in a moment. "Jamey didn't really scare you did he?"

She thought back to what had happened right after Jamey spoke. There was a gun, a real one, not a toy. And there was a filthy red bandanna. Someone was wearing it, but not Jamey. "No. Jamey didn't scare me. But something kind of . . . disturbed me."

Tom looked at her with alarm. "Did you remember something?" His voice was hoarse.

"I think so, but I don't know what it means." She started to blurt out that she had seen a man wearing a bandanna and holding a gun. But something made her stop. A gun! The words of Sheriff Gulch rang in her mind: *There's a crime ring in this county, and I think she's at the center of it.* The man with the gun might be her partner in crime. Or, more likely, was she his victim?

She glanced up into Tom's trusting eyes and panic seized her. Was the sheriff right after all? Was she a criminal?

Nine

"You said something upset you," Tom said with concern. "What was it?"

"I-I don't know," she lied. "Listen, um, do you mind if I lie down for a while? I'm feeling a little shaky all of the sudden."

"Of course I don't mind. The pie can wait. And don't worry about making lunch either. I'll make us some sandwiches later. Now go lie down."

Tom led her slowly up the stairs and to her bedroom door. "Rest. Sleep if you can. Tell me if you start feeling worse, and we'll call the doctor. I won't go out in the field again until I'm convinced you're going to be all right."

She nodded and went to sit on the bed. Tom started to go, but paused as she kicked off her shoes, his huge frame filling the doorway. "If you want to talk about anything, anything at all, I'll be just a shout away."

She lay down on the cool cotton quilt and listened to his footsteps fade out as he went down the hall. She tried to rest, but her mind swirled with a thousand thoughts and fears. Who was the man with the gun?

Was this the man whose ring she'd worn? If she took out ads in the newspaper, as Tom had suggested, would this man come to claim her and take her back to a life of crime? Or something worse? She sat up and fluffed her pillow, punching it fiercely before settling her head back onto it. She couldn't be a criminal. She just knew it!

She curled up on her side and squeezed her eyes shut. If all this weren't enough to think about, there was the added stress of dealing with Tom after what had happened under the apple tree. She'd like nothing better right now than to run to those sheltering arms where she'd felt so secure. The whole situation brought home the difficulty of the "hands off" agreement they had made.

As she pondered all this, exhaustion finally overtook her, and she fell into a troubled sleep. She dreamt of a journey filled with wild and dangerous farm animals who lay in wait for her at every turn. Surly, threatening appliances opened their mechanical maws to snap at her heels. She ran from them for her life, only to be confronted by a man wearing a bandanna . . . and holding a gun.

Dorothy awoke with a start, swallowed hard and rubbed her eyes. At that moment, she knew that her fears would haunt her until she got them off her chest. She had to tell Tom everything.

After splashing water on her face and brushing her hair, she went downstairs. Tom was at his desk, doing his never-ending paperwork.

He looked up from punching numbers into a calculator and gave her a concerned smile. "You're looking more like your old self again. How are you feeling?"

"Better," she said, and wondered if it was true. "I need to talk to you about something. Where's Jamey?"

He got up from the desk and came toward her slowly. He'd obviously heard the tension in her voice. "Outside playing. He won't disturb us. What's wrong?"

When he was within arm's reach of her, she strode away from him toward the window. If he took her hands again, or worse yet, took her in his arms, she'd never get through what she had to say. And she had to say what was on her mind, for his and Jamey's sake.

"Tom, you said before that I could tell you anything. Do you mean that?"

"That's right," he said cautiously. "Anything. There's nothing you can tell me that I won't understand."

She thought about what he'd told her under the apple tree when he'd apologized for being tactless. He might see himself that way, but he could be so understanding and sweet when he wanted to be. She crossed her arms and rubbed them as a sudden chill crept up her spine. "What I have to tell you is about what disturbed me earlier in the kitchen."

"Yes?"

"It was this, this vision." She heard him coming toward her again and she turned her back to him entirely. She had to get through this.

"What was it?" His voice was soft, little more than a whisper.

"It was a man with a gun. He was wearing a bandanna around his head. I think I know him, and I think he's bad, maybe even a robber or something." She put her hand to her mouth briefly to calm herself. "Oh, Tom, I'm afraid I might be a . . . a . . . gun moll."

She jumped, startled, as Tom burst into laughter. Whirling around, she saw that he had collapsed into the easy chair, his hands clasped across his chest. She gaped at him, shocked and annoyed that he could find her predicament funny.

"Gun moll! The last time I heard that term, it was in an old Jimmy Cagney movie. That's a good one. Where in the hell did you get that idea?"

"I just told you! I saw a familiar man, he was bad, and he had a gun."

Tom sprawled lazily across the chair, and slung a long leg over one of its overstuffed arms. "Honey, it's probably just something you saw on television. What makes you think he's someone you know?"

"Because it's not the only vision I've had lately, that's why."

Tom's expression became wary, and his eyes lost their laughter. "What others have you had?"

Dorothy told him about the cook and the man leading the horse and her conviction that they were people she knew in her former life. "At first I thought the man teaching me to ride was my father, so I got all excited. Then you suggested that he was only a hired instructor, and it kind of burst my bubble. That's why I got angry with you yesterday. I know that wasn't fair. Sorry."

"That's okay," Tom said quietly, his dark brows knit together. She could tell he was thinking about the implications of what she'd told him, maybe about how her visions of hired help gave credence to his "rich girl" theory. "Well, it looks like your memory might be starting to come back." He smiled a smile that didn't reach his eyes. "I wouldn't worry too much about the man with the gun, though. There could be a hundred explanations for it. Maybe he was someone teaching you to shoot or something."

Dorothy squared her shoulders. Tom obviously wasn't taking this seriously enough. "There's something else I need to tell you. Do you remember when Sheriff Gulch came out here the morning after you brought me here?"

Tom nodded and leaned his head back against the chair. He was trying to look casual and relaxed, but she sensed that he was as tense as she.

"Well, I overheard everything he said that day. I know he thinks I'm a criminal and that I was part of some crime wave or something."

Tom looked down for a moment, evidently letting this information sink in. Then he looked back at her and smiled. "I'll bet you've been worrying about that all this time, haven't you?"

Dorothy nodded.

"Well, there you are. That's the answer." Tom stood up, waving one hand in the air as if he'd just solved the whole puzzle.

"What do you mean?"

"You've been obsessing about that since the day Gulch was out here, and your subconscious mind probably just conjured up an image in response to that. That and having Jamey surprise you like he did. You've got to admit, the part about him wearing a bandanna like some Old West gunslinger is pretty corny. Your subconscious just produced a stereotyped image of a bad guy based on every western movie you've ever seen."

She blinked, warming to this idea. "Do you really think so?"

"Absolutely. Gulch is a clown anyway. Don't let anything he says upset you."

Tom's optimism was infectious. Though she still had doubts, she realized he could actually be right. In fact, he probably was right. Overcome by gratitude for the ray of hope he'd given her, she stepped forward and hugged him. "Thank you. I feel so much better now."

His arms encircled her and pressed her to him. "There's no way I believe you could rob anyone, steal from anyone, or deliberately hurt anyone. It's just not in you. Whoever you are, you're a good woman."

She pressed her cheek to his chest and inhaled his warm man's scent. She could feel the crisp hair in the open V at the neck of his shirt, and need for him flared deep inside her as it had yesterday under the apple tree. It seemed that neither of them breathed as tension flowed between their yearning bodies. Not only were their bodies fairly humming with the same vibrations of desire, but their minds were in sync as well. At the same time, they each remembered the vow they made some twenty-four hours before, and gently, reluctantly, pulled away from each other.

"Thanks for listening. What you said makes a lot of sense." She could still see the smoky traces of passion in his hooded eyes.

"You're welcome."

"Well, I'm feeling fine now, so I guess I'll go and finish making that pie." She left him and headed to the kitchen. With one last glance over her shoulder, she saw that he was looking after her like a man dying of thirst. She felt pretty thirsty herself.

Tom watched her leave the room, his mind in turmoil. When she was out of sight, he collapsed into the easy chair again and released a long, pent-up breath. It was finally happening—her memory was creeping back little by little. It validated the wisdom of their agreement not to get involved with each other, but it didn't make it easier to bear. When he'd touched her just now, it was all he could do to keep from kissing her again like he had yesterday. Now he felt as if the warmth was draining from his body.

He rubbed his temple, reflecting on what she had said about her visions, as she had called them. The mysterious man with the gun would probably turn out to be no more than a character from a movie she'd once seen. The episode did, however, remind him that he hadn't spoken to Sheriff Gulch since the day he'd come out to the farm, and that was some time ago.

He'd figured the sheriff would let him know if he learned anything new about Dorothy's situation. It was just possible, though, that Gulch had gotten busy with other things and put her case on the back burner. Part of him had wished that were true, the same part that had begun to wish that Dorothy could stay on the farm with him and Jamey forever. But now that her memory seemed to be returning bit by bit, there was no sense delaying the inevitable. It couldn't hurt to call the station just to touch base.

He retrieved the phone book from the bottom shelf

of the end table beside him and looked up the number of the sheriff's office. With his fingers poised above the phone's keypad, he hesitated. What if the sheriff told him something he didn't want to hear? He mentally steeled himself and dialed.

"Gulch here," the sheriff said after the receptionist put Tom through.

"This is Tom Weaver. I'm just calling to see if you've turned up anything new in Dorothy's—er, the missing woman's case."

"Nope, 'fraid not. I haven't turned up a single clue since we talked last, but I did get a lead on a women's shelter that's willing to take her as soon as a space opens up. I still recommend that, Tom."

Tom bristled and bit back a sharp reply. The man was only doing his job after all. "I don't think that's going to be necessary. She's starting to get some of her memories back. It may not be long until she knows who she is."

"Is that right?" The sheriff's tone was heavy with sarcasm. "You don't mean to tell me that you're still buying into that amnesia story."

Tom gritted his teeth. "Yes, I still believe she's telling the truth."

"You know that theory I had about her being in on the crime wave we've been having? Well, I think so now more than ever. You wanna know why?"

"Sure." But he wasn't sure, not at all. A chilly wave of apprehension gripped his gut.

"Immediately after you took that girl out to the farm, the crimes just stopped. We haven't had an armed robbery or a burglary in the county of that particular M.O.

since you've had her cooped up out there on your place. It's no coincidence, Tom. I would strongly advise you to let me get her into that women's shelter as soon as possible. Then she'll be someone else's problem."

Tom thought he heard himself thank the sheriff for his time before he hung up the phone. It was a damned coincidence, that was all. Whoever was responsible for the crimes had just happened to move on about the time Dorothy came. That had to be the answer.

He stood and walked to the bay window where he could see Jamey playing in the yard. He was still in full cowboy regalia—hat, gunbelt, and boots. Except now Toto was sporting the red bandanna around his scrawny neck. As he watched the boy brandish the toy gun at an invisible foe, an achy spot formed in his throat as it did sometimes when he watched his son during a happy moment. He wished with all his heart that nothing would ever spoil that happiness.

Happy moments had been hard to come by in the months since Jamey's mother had left, but now they were the norm, thanks to Dorothy. Tom thought he usually knew what was best for his son, and protecting a five-year-old seemed mostly simple. But telling him not to get attached to Dorothy wasn't as easy as telling him not to run with scissors. Was it possible that she was really involved in some dangerous element that might eventually hurt Jamey? If she had been mixed up with criminals, what were the chances that they would come for her some day? And cause trouble when they did?

He saw the old hound lift its hind foot to scratch at the bandanna, which he evidently found disagreeable. As he pawed at it, the bandanna spun around and around his neck comically. Tom was suddenly hit with the sensation of having lost his stomach, as if he were on a roller coaster. *The bandanna.* Why hadn't he thought of it while he was talking to the sheriff?

Tom went back to the phone, and after a moment's hesitation, hit the redial button. Once again, he was put through to the sheriff. "Harvey, it's Tom Weaver again. I meant to ask you before if you had any descriptions of those armed robbers you mentioned."

"There were two of them—a tall guy and a short guy. I know where you're going with this," Gulch said defensively. "Just because we didn't get a report of a woman doesn't mean she wasn't involved. She could have been the getaway man, er, woman. Or even the mastermind."

Tom squeezed his eyes shut and tried not to snap at the man at the end of the line. "Harvey, the two men— what did they look like?"

"We weren't able to get enough facial descriptions to do a drawing because one wore a ski mask and the other wore a bandanna across his face."

Gulch's words slammed Tom like a blow to the solar plexus. "That's all I wanted to know. Thanks."

Tom's mouth went dry as an icy fear settled over his heart. He stood again and paced the room, jamming both hands into his unruly hair. Through his shock, he commanded himself to calm down and analyze the situation rationally. A half hour ago, Dorothy had been confessing to being a gun moll, as she had so amusingly put it. If she was really a bad person, why would she have so readily admitted to something incriminating, based on nothing but a fleeting vision of a bad man with a gun and a bandanna? No, it didn't make sense. She was honest and decent. He knew it. He felt it. And if she'd gotten involved with criminals through no fault of her own, it only meant she needed his help even more.

Just as he'd promised himself he wouldn't get emotionally involved with her, he was being drawn down deeper into her problems, which could eventually put his son at risk. But he couldn't abandon her, not when she looked at him with those trusting blue eyes. He'd give her a home, and probably his heart. Then someday the man she'd belonged to would come, and she'd turn those very eyes on the stranger with recognition and love. And then she'd be gone. Tom sank into the easy chair and hung his head.

Dorothy opened the gate and made her way carefully to the Hog House, watching her every step to make sure she got none of the muck on her shoes. Glinda the pig was having grave complications delivering her first litter. Dorothy wished she had better news from the vet, but it wasn't to be. She dreaded the look on Jamey's face when she told him.

"Doc Reynolds's office called back. They said he's halfway across the county on another emergency. He can't get here before morning." The two didn't look up when she spoke, but as she came closer, she saw the worry on their faces.

"Glinda might last that long," Tom said. "But her pigs won't."

The panting animal was so exhausted, she was barely struggling. Dorothy couldn't stand to watch the animal suffer, and she looked away. This young sow was in her prime. She was tame, almost a pet, and Jamey loved her.

"I raised her since she was this big," the boy said sadly, holding out his chubby hands five or six inches apart. He blinked back tears, trying to be brave.

"Isn't there anything we can do?" Dorothy looked pleadingly at Tom.

Tom turned his head and regarded her intently for a moment, as if trying to make up his mind about something. After a quick glance at Jamey, he took her arm and led her out of his earshot. "There's nothing Jamey or I can do."

"What do you mean?"

"I mean, my arms are too big, and although his are slender, they're not strong enough."

It took a moment for his meaning to sink in, and when it did, a wave of revulsion washed over her. "You don't mean you want me to . . . to . . ."

He read her expression and breathed a defeated sigh. "It was a crazy thing to ask. It's enough that you cook and clean and watch Jamey for the pittance I pay you. I can't ask you to be a midwife for a sow in the bargain. Forget it. Don't give it another thought."

She watched him walk back to Jamey's side, and then looked down at her white tennis shoes, which she had just gone to such pains to keep clean. If she did as Tom asked, she'd be in for a lot more than a little grime on her shoes. A little shiver of disgust rattled her, and her eyes settled on Jamey again, the very picture of sorrow.

She squared her shoulders. If there was anything she could do to prevent Jamey from losing a beloved pet, wild pigs couldn't stop her. What did a little dirt and slime matter in the grand scheme of the universe anyway?

She thrust out her chin and began rolling up her shirt sleeves. "Jamey," she called out. The boy and his father looked up at her with cautious hope. She was struck again by how much Jamey looked like Tom, especially when they wore identical expressions, as they did now. "I want you to go to the house and bring me a bar of soap and a pail of hot water. Doctor Dorothy is going to deliver some pigs."

Later that night, Tom was in the kitchen alone. The teapot squealed, but he didn't hear it although he was standing right over it. He was too lost in thoughts of Dorothy. When the billowing steam reached his eyes, he blinked and turned off the stove. She'd amazed him tonight. He couldn't possibly thank her for what she'd done, but he had to at least try. The delicate aroma of orange and spices wafted up to him as he poured boiling water over the tea bag nestled in the fragile china cup.

He hated like hell to put her through that ordeal. Not only was delivering pigs dirty work, but her arm, back, and shoulders had taken a beating. If she'd felt any discomfort, though, she never complained. How could he ever have doubted her character or her constitution? After what he'd seen tonight, he believed she could withstand any test farm life had to offer.

Only one doubt haunted him, and it was the biggest doubt of all. How soon would her former life, her *real* life, come to take her from him? He'd agreed to keep his distance, but after the strength of character she'd shown tonight, his resolve was waning. He wanted her more than ever. His control was slipping badly, and right now, he felt as if anything could happen.

Dorothy emerged from a hot bath all flushed and glowing, still exhilarated by her accomplishment. She'd soaked and scrubbed until she felt that she'd surely never been cleaner in her life. She wrapped herself in the thick terry robe Tom had given her, wound her hair up in a soft towel, and crossed the hall to her bedroom. Everything was still and quiet. She thought she'd heard the teapot earlier, but that was probably just the weather vane squeaking again.

Jamey had gone to bed as soon as they'd come back. He'd been as excited as she was, and almost as exhausted. She'd been wrong the time she'd thought it wasn't a good idea to let him watch the birth. The look of wonder on his face was priceless. Tom's instincts about what his son could handle had been right on target. She admired him all the more. He'd said little but a brief "thank you" after they'd returned to the house, and had probably gone to bed. She glanced longingly at his closed door before entering her own bedroom.

She unwound the towel from her hair and let the damp, curly mass fall around her shoulders. Tom was probably disgusted by what she'd had to do—he seemed that way anyway. It had all been worth it, though, just to see Jamey's face as she'd delivered each wriggling piglet into the world. Despite her revulsion and all the discomfort, she felt proud of what she'd accomplished. And not just for what it meant to Tom and Jamey, but for what it meant to her. She'd proven to herself that she could take on any hardship that came her way and meet it head-on. As her fingers closed around her hairbrush on the vanity table, a spasm in her hand caused her to wince.

A soft knock sounded at her door. "Can I come in?" Her pulse leapt at the sound of Tom's voice.

Surprised and pleased that he had come to check on her, she tightened the sash of her robe and smoothed her hair as best she could. "Come in."

Tom opened the door, balancing a wooden tray with his other hand. "I thought you might be hungry after all the work you did tonight, Doctor Dorothy." He crossed the room to where she stood and set the tray on the vanity table.

On the tray was a cup of tea, a sandwich, and a delicate rose, which he'd evidently cut from the garden and set afloat in a small crystal bowl. She recognized the cup as part of the good china that was kept in the dining room cupboard.

"Wow, I'm impressed. You even cut the crusts off the bread." She smiled up at him teasingly. "I didn't think men ever did that."

He smiled self-consciously and looked away. "They do when they want things to be special for someone. I hope you like the sandwich. It's cream cheese and pineapple. That's my mother's favorite."

She took a bite. "Wonderful," she said and meant it, "but you didn't have to go to all this trouble."

"Yes, I did. It took a lot of courage to do what you did tonight. And a lot of character. You should be very proud of yourself—I know I'm proud of you."

Tom stuffed his hands into his pockets as if he didn't know what else to do with them. Dorothy had never seen him act this way before. This exhibition of schoolboy shyness on the part of the big, strong, usually self-assured man was very becoming, she thought. Very becoming indeed. Suddenly thirsty, she picked up the teacup, but it clattered back into the saucer after she'd raised it only a couple of inches. She winced and grasped her throbbing hand with the other.

Tom stepped forward, concern creasing his brow. He took her hand and pressed it into his own huge palm, massaging it with his big, blunt fingers until the spasm eased. She caught her bottom lip between her teeth as the tension that had left her hand spread throughout the rest of her body. She could feel the roughness of his skin in her every nerve ending and was keenly aware of her nakedness beneath the robe. As he continued to stroke her hand, her skin came alive and she felt she could feel every loop in the nubby terrycloth.

"Poor Dorothy." His voice was soft, a low, masculine purr like that of a big jungle cat. "You're going to be sore tomorrow." Both his powerful hands moved up her arm in a firm, kneading massage. "How's that feel?"

"Ah. Ah. Wonderful," she rasped. "Don't forget my neck. It hurts most of all." He put his hands on her shoulders and drew her to him. The pressure of his fingertips was both soothing and electrifying. While he pressed on the muscles of her back, he also pressed her intimately closer to his body. "I was afraid you'd be . . . you know, disgusted by what I had to do."

His dark brows arched upwards, and he leaned so close she could feel his warm breath on her face. "Oh, no. If I didn't have much to say, it was just because I felt so bad that you had to go through all that. I felt guilty I even asked you, but I had to for Jamey's sake." His green eyes looked as deep as the ocean. "I never want to do anything that causes you pain. Rest your head on my chest and try to relax." He probed her taut neck muscles gently.

Try to relax, he says. While she could feel each and every muscle from his chest to his thighs? Not likely. White-hot desire spread through her body as he pressed her to him. She wrapped her arms around him and flattened her cheek against his hard pectoral muscles. He felt like heaven. She could have been able to hear his heart if her own were not thundering in her ears. She felt his arms come around her, molding their torsos together in an embrace so powerful she thought she'd lose her breath.

He put one hand gently under her chin and raised her face, but instead of covering her mouth with his own as she longed for him to do, he stared at her wildly, his eyes black with desire. "I don't know what to do anymore. I thought if I could keep you at arm's length I wouldn't fall in love with you. But it's too late for that. I'm already there, and I'm going to be devastated if you leave, *when* you leave. I'm lost, no matter what. So tell me, Dorothy. What do we do now? My heart is in your hands."

Ten

She looked into his eyes, so full of need, pleading for guidance, and she realized that she *did* know what they should do. She might not know who she'd been before she came here, but she knew who she was now. And looking at Tom, she realized that she knew what she wanted.

"I'm not going to leave. No matter what my old life was before I came here, it's just that—my *old* life. Even if there was a man in my life before, I can't have loved him as much as I love you."

He released a pent-up breath and made a noise that was part sigh and part moan. She could see that her words had touched him, but his eyes lost none of their desperation. "But you don't know what you might be giving up. You might have a wonderful life. One that doesn't include backbreaking work from sunup until sundown."

"I don't care about that. I want to stay here on the farm as long as you'll let me." She paused and pushed herself a step farther away from him. "And I want to be with you now. Tonight."

As he watched, breathless, her slender hands went to the sash of the robe and slowly worked it loose. The robe parted slightly, and she eased one creamy thigh through the opening. An audible groan escaped his lips as she pulled the robe away from her body, down her shoulders and let it drop to the floor in a heap.

His eyes took in the sight of her hungrily and then he pulled her to him. Trapping a mass of damp, curly hair behind her head, he guided her face to his and captured her lips in a demanding kiss. His hand went to the curve of her bottom and pressed her hard against him. She could feel his desire for her in all the rigid planes of his body.

Dorothy worked one hand between them and began to undo his shirt buttons, one by one. When he released her to finish shrugging off the shirt, she went to the bed and turned back the covers. She turned around to face him again, and her breath caught in her throat. His skin was bronzed to perfection, defining each and every ropy muscle in his arms and chest. He came to her and captured her in yet another embrace, then lifted her onto the bed, laying her down with one smooth motion, following her body with his own.

He covered every inch of her neck and shoulders with kisses that made her whole body quiver, while her hands roamed his back and chest. The washboard-hard muscles of his abdomen, covered with a mat of crisp black curls, rippled and flexed at her touch. She moaned and arched her body against his as he found her breasts and began a slow, thorough massage from the outsides to the sensitive buds of her nipples.

Just as she thought she couldn't bear any more, he

shifted his body, lowering his mouth to her breasts and his hands to her thighs. She cried out as his tongue swirled around the rosy, taut peaks of her breasts. Squeezing her eyes tightly shut, the exquisite sensations almost too much to bear, she heard herself moan as swirling colors filled her brain and her breath came in hitching rasps.

As she cradled his head in her hands, her fingers weaving through the silky strands of his thick, blue-black waves, she wondered, had any other man ever done this to her? Had anyone ever made her feel like this? No. Impossible. How could she ever have forgotten?

His hand slipped gently between her thighs, sending new, blinding sensations through her and making her cry out. She knew instinctively that if he continued to touch her this way, she would soon be unable to speak. She forced her eyes open and breathlessly, while she still could, she whispered, "As of today, the past is gone. My life begins again, here and now. You're my first, my one and only."

The look of love in his eyes made her heart melt. Her hands went to his waist and she unfastened his jeans, freeing his straining body. He shucked off the jeans and kissed her once more. Then he eased himself between her thighs and joined them, whispering tender words she could not understand, because all thought had left her, and only sensation remained. The wind picked up outside and the gossamer curtains swayed rhythmically, as if keeping time with the movement of their bodies. Gentle rain began to patter on the roof, but she was unaware of anything but his hoarse, raspy moans, musky scent, and the feel of his skin against hers.

She felt herself riding the crest of a wave that broke in a shattering burst of emotion. She clung to him tightly and could feel that he was with her at the peak, and they stayed there together until they were finally sated and lay exhausted in each other's arms.

He circled her body with one arm and cradled her head against his shoulder. With his free hand, he stroked her still damp hair, smoothing it away from her face. She rubbed her cheek against him, loving the feel of the coarse hair against her skin. She opened her eyes and saw a two-inch scar along his collarbone. Tracing it lightly with her finger she asked, "What happened here?"

"Old football injury," he said, his voice a breathy whisper. "Broken collarbone."

She leaned forward and kissed it, running her tongue along the smooth, jagged surface of the scar. "There. All well again."

His arms went around her tightly, pressing her head firmly to his chest. She could feel his breath quicken, his heart pick up speed. "Can you heal all my scars with your kisses, Doctor Dorothy?"

She wanted to raise her face to his, to look in his eyes and try to read what he was feeling, but she could not because he was holding her so tightly. "Yes. I can," she said, her lips brushing his neck lightly. She fervently hoped that she really could heal his scars, especially the ones you couldn't see, the ones on the inside.

He drew in a ragged breath. "I believe you can. But I want you to know something." He paused, as if gathering his thoughts, or his courage, or both. He tenderly took her hand and pressed it to his lips for a moment before he continued. "What you said about staying with me, no matter what. I'm not going to hold you to it. If the time ever comes when it's best for you to leave, then you should leave. Before it's too late."

"Don't say that!" She tried to raise her head again, but he pressed it more firmly to his chest. He evidently didn't want her to look at him, at least not until he was finished. And what did he mean by "before it's too late?" Too late for what?

"No. Just listen. I want you to feel free. Free enough so that you can always do what's best for you, no matter what. Will you promise me that?"

She sighed. "Yes. I promise." She closed her eyes and relaxed against him. It was an easy promise to make, after all. Because she knew that what was best for her, what would always be best, would be to stay with him. No matter what her past turned out to be.

Tom planted the pitchfork in the hay and leaned against it to rest. A warm spell made the barn seem hot and airless even though it was early evening. Light from the setting sun streamed through one of the doors, illuminating motes of dust and bits of hay as they swirled through the humid air.

Tom's eyelids drooped slowly closed and the lovely image of Dorothy came into his mind, her hair spread out on her pillow like a delicate fan. Her arms reaching out to him. His eyes flew open again as Hickory the bull let loose a bellow from his nearby stall.

"All right, all right. Here, take this, you big crybaby." Tom speared a forkful of new-mown hay and pitched it to the bull, then yawned and stretched and sat down on a small barrel. He'd almost fallen asleep standing up just now, and he didn't have to ask himself why. It had been a week since he and Dorothy had first been together, and he had gone to her bedroom every night since then after Jamey was in bed. Their spirited lovemaking had gone on late into the night, leaving him exhausted but more fulfilled than he'd ever been at any time in his life. Just the thought of her brought a smile to his lips and a warm glow to his heart.

Dorothy seemed happy and content too, and for that he was glad. Their newfound intimacy seemed to give her even more confidence in herself and her future. But for him, the future loomed ahead like a dark tunnel. And while Dorothy seemed to be able to see a light at the end, he couldn't help wondering if that light was the headlamp of an oncoming train. He wanted to be able to believe her when she said she'd stay no matter what the future brought. The defense mechanism he'd built around his heart wouldn't let him believe, but it couldn't stop him from the freefall into love with the wonderful woman who, it seemed, had come from heaven itself. But everyone knew the Lord giveth and He taketh away. Each time he took her in his arms could be the very last time.

"You look serious."

He looked up to see Dorothy regarding him thoughtfully. She'd brought Jamey's boom box with her and set it down on a table against the far wall of the barn. Lord, what that woman could do for jeans and a T-shirt, he thought, his eyes taking in her small waist and the womanly curve of her hips and breasts. It seemed as if the air in the barn had just gotten a few degrees hotter and his jeans a size smaller. He waved his hand dismissively. "It's nothing."

Her elegant brows drew together for a second and she pointed at Hickory. "What's *he* doing in here?"

"I had to fasten him up in his stall so he'll be ready to go back to Taylor's farm tomorrow. Do you remember when he went there a while back to, er, *dance* with some of the cows?"

Dorothy nodded, a sly grin tugging at the corners of her mouth.

"Well, it seems that he didn't get the job completely done. So he has to go back."

She gave the bull a smug look. "Couldn't cut the mustard, eh?" Hickory stared at her sullenly as he chewed, straw sticking out from both sides of his mouth like a bristly beard.

"So it would seem."

"Do you know what I think?"

"No. What?"

"I think he needs a real man to show him how it's done." Dorothy reached for the controls of the boom box and turned it on. The soulful strains of Eric Clapton's "Wonderful Tonight" filled the space between them like a physical, beckoning presence.

Dorothy started toward him slowly, and with a wink of one azure blue eye said, "Wanna *dance?"*

Tom got to his feet and went to meet her. When they came together, she draped her arms around his neck as he encircled her with his own. They swayed to the sultry music, their bodies pressed together, their gazes locked. "By the way, where's Jamey? I'd hate for him to wander in here when we were in the midst of, ah, dancing."

"Don't worry. He's ensconced in front of the TV. He's started *The Wizard of Oz* over from the beginning, and I told him he could watch it all the way through."

Tom chuckled. "Good thinking. But I thought you didn't believe in using a VCR as a baby-sitter." He pulled her closer and let one hand drop to cup her denim-clad bottom and squeeze it gently.

"Ordinarily I don't, but I decided to make an exception. Besides, how else are we going to make sure that he doesn't move for two hours?"

"Two hours!" Tom exclaimed in mock alarm. "I'm glad I took my vitamins this morning."

Her eyes widened. "I'm glad too."

Slowly, Tom began to dance Dorothy toward the mound of hay in the corner of the barn. "Ever had a roll in the hay?"

"Not that I can remember. But there's a first time for everything."

Clad in a cotton slip, Dorothy sprayed starch on the fabric spread out on the ironing board, which she now kept in her room by the sewing machine. She worked the tip of the iron painstakingly along the jumper's shoulder strap. "Ow!" She yelped as the iron's point slid over her index finger with which she'd been holding down the material. Waving her hand frantically in the air, she decided she'd better quit ironing before there were any more injuries. Her ironing wasn't much better than her vacuuming or her dishwasher loading. She unplugged the iron and stuck her finger in the glass of iced tea she'd put on the vanity table. Then she went to lie on the bed for a moment until the throbbing eased.

She needed a break anyway. She'd gotten Jamey's costume done just in time and had already gotten him suited up and his whiskers painted on for the masquerade ball. Then all she'd had to do was get herself ready, but now that task would be more difficult with a throbbing finger. She put the finger in her mouth and tried to relax for a moment. She looked up to see the breeze from the window flutter the canopy over her head and thought of the last few nights here in this bed with Tom. A burning sensation spread all over her body, and it wasn't from the seared finger, but from the memory of Tom and how he'd made love to her.

She understood that life on the farm meant a lot of ups and downs. But she could cope with whatever came her way as long as she had Tom and his love and support. She examined her finger and saw that a blister was forming. So what if she still had mishaps from time to time? The way Tom made her feel made everything worth it.

After a moment, she got up and went to the mirror, holding up the blue-and-white gingham jumper. It wouldn't get any raves for seamstressing from Martha Stewart, but it wasn't bad. And it should be a good way to break the ice with the people she'd meet tonight.

At the sound of a knock on the door, she started and clasped the jumper to her chest.

"Thirty minutes until showtime," Tom said in a teasing voice. "I know this is supposed to be a surprise,

but I don't think I can wait for it anymore. I'm coming
in." He rattled the old-fashioned glass doorknob and
laughed wickedly. "Are you decent?"

"No!"

"Good." He rattled the knob again.

"Don't you dare come in here!" Dorothy sprang toward the closet and quickly hung up the jumper and
closed the closet door. She didn't want Tom to see her
in the costume until she'd done her hair and makeup,
so that she could make her big entrance down the staircase and give him the full effect. Still, the deep rum-
blings of his masculine laughter on the other side of
the door were becoming too much for her to bear. Perhaps it wouldn't hurt to let him help braid her hair,
particularly since her injured hand was now so sore she
wasn't sure she could manage to do it on her own.

"Aw, c'mon," he begged. "Jamey's already got his
lion's costume on and he's been terrorizing the dog for
the last half hour. That was fun for a while, but now
I'm bored with it. Are you sure there aren't any buttons
I can button or zippers I can zip?"

Dorothy went to the door and pulled it open. "I
thought your specialty was *un*buttoning and *un*zipping."

Tom took a deep breath and let his gaze roam shame-
lessly over her body. She could feel her breasts tighten
under his frank scrutiny beneath the flimsy cotton slip.
Tom stepped into the room beside her and shut the door.

"Ah, so you appreciate my magic fingers, do you?
You're right. Unbuttoning and unzipping are my special-
ties, but the skill I'm most proud of is the old one-
handed bra unhook." He reached around her back, and
she danced away from him lithely.

"Hey! I thought you said we only had thirty minutes to get ready. If you want us to leave on time, you'd better keep your magic fingers off my bra and bring them over here to help me do my hair."

Tom looked skeptical. "Well, ma'am, I've been accused of being a lot of things in my time, but a hairdresser's not one of 'em."

"All you have to do is braid it. That shouldn't be too hard for a guy who can unhook a bra with one hand."

"Oh, is that all? Why, I'm an old hand at hair braiding."

She gave him a suspicious look. "Is that right?"

"Sure. I used to braid horses' tails for horse shows all the time."

"Well that does make me feel better," she said, making a face. She sat down on the vanity seat in front of the mirror and handed him a brush. He took it with a grin and began to brush her hair in long, slow strokes. The sensation of his hands on her hair sent ripples of pleasure down her spine. "So tell me," she began haltingly, closing her eyes. "How many hours of your formative adolescent years were spent in the back seat of cars perfecting your unhooking technique?"

"Surprisingly few," he said, his voice coming to her as a raspy whisper. "I was a quick study. And then there's my natural ability." He picked up a comb and began to part her hair in the middle, smoothing it down carefully on both sides with his fingers.

"Hmmm. I know a little something about your natural abilities. And now you can add hairdressing to your long list of talents."

"It's nice to know I have something to fall back on.

But I'm a little surprised you wanted me to help you. I thought you were saving your whole masquerade look as a surprise."

"I was. But then I ironed my finger and it's too sore to braid with." She held up her reddened finger.

"Poor baby," Tom cooed. "I know you women go to a lot of trouble to look your best, and I've heard of ironing your hair, but this is a little extreme."

"Very funny." She laughed and allowed him to take her hand gently and examine her throbbing finger.

"It's blistering already." He brought her hand to his mouth and lightly brushed her finger with his lips. "All better?"

She sighed and leaned her head back against him, thrilling to his touch. "Much."

He released her hand and bent down to press a kiss to the nape of her neck. "You know that thirty-minute time frame I mentioned a little while ago?"

"Yes." She stopped breathing as his hands moved downward from her neck. He hooked his thumbs underneath the straps of her slip and bra, lowering them with maddening slowness over her shoulders.

"I think it would be permissible for Princess Dorothy of the Netherlands to be fashionably late."

An hour later, Tom waited at the bottom of the staircase, his Sunday Stetson in his hand, with Jamey at his side. He patted the boy's lion ears and smoothed down the fabric fringe that formed his mane. Jamey's eyes remained riveted on the staircase as he waited for

Dorothy's entrance. When they saw her, Jamey squealed with delight and Tom's deep laughter filled the foyer.

"You look just like the Dorothy in the movie!" Jamey exclaimed, jumping up and down so vigorously that his lion's tail wagged.

"I should say you do, all the way down to your ruby slippers." He looked down at Dorothy's pumps, the ones he'd found her in, and grinned.

"Well, they might not be ruby slippers exactly, but snakeskin will have to do."

"Snakeskin! Cool!" Jamey stared at the shoes, gaping.

"I'll say one thing for you," Tom said. "Nobody will be able to accuse you of not having a sense of humor."

Eleven

The corn festival had elements of a county fair, a swap meet, and a costume party. Dorothy and Tom strolled the midway watching people try to win the impossible arcade games, listening to the barkers, and trying to help Jamey keep his cotton candy out of his fur.

Dorothy's and Jamey's costumes elicited smiles and favorable comments from people Tom knew and strangers alike. Two of the friends Tom introduced her to said they had heard that Dorothy was royalty of some kind. "Princess Dorothy of the Netherlands! Clyde the gossip hound strikes again!" Tom had said, hooting with laughter.

After accepting compliments from one of Tom's friends for her costume, she told Tom, "Now, aren't you sorry you didn't wear one yourself, spoilsport?" She pinched off a piece of Jamey's cotton candy and popped it into her mouth. The wispy confection melted on her tongue in a cherry-flavored rush.

"Yeah, I always hate to pass up an opportunity to look silly in front of my fellow farmers," Tom deadpanned, watching her lick the sugary residue from the candy off her fingers. "How's the cotton candy? It's been years since I had any."

Jamey's attention was diverted by the colorful cups and saucers spinning away on a nearby ride, so Dorothy reached down to pluck some of the candy from its paper spindle. "Not like that," Tom said, slipping an arm around her. "Like this." He pressed a kiss to her mouth and swirled his tongue across her lips. "Mmm. Good."

When he'd released her, Dorothy blushed, surprised by Tom's public display of affection. She looked around to see if anyone was watching them, but the other festival-goers were too busy to notice.

"This is the spring corn festival," Tom said, observing her bashfulness. "It's like the county fair, only it celebrates the bounty of nature busting out all over. A certain amount of sparking and spooning on the midway is part of the tradition." He winked at her wolfishly before turning his attention to Jamey, who'd begun tugging on his sleeve asking to ride the cup and saucers.

"I thought it was to celebrate the end of planting season," Dorothy said skeptically.

"Same difference."

As Tom dug into his jeans pocket for change for the ride, Dorothy realized that something she'd just said about the end of planting season made her vaguely troubled. Then she remembered. Tom had once promised her that after planting season was over, they would redouble their efforts to find out her identity. He'd been too busy and in too much need of help with Jamey to make it a high priority until then. He'd promised her that after planting was over, he'd take her to the university or anywhere else she wanted to go to look for anything familiar. At first she'd looked forward to finding out who she was, but things were so different now. Would finding her old life disrupt her life with Tom and Jamey?

She stood at Tom's side, his arm draped around her casually, as they watched Jamey on the carnival ride. As the cups weaved and spun, Jamey would disappear from sight for a moment, only to swing back into view, shrieking and giggling. There one moment, gone the next. A sudden, powerful ache gripped Dorothy's heart and she leaned toward Tom, resting her head on his granite-hard chest.

"Are you okay?" Tom looked at her with concern. The light from a Japanese lantern strung overhead made his eyes an otherworldly blue.

"Watching the cups and saucers got me a little dizzy for a second." She managed what she hoped was a convincing smile and squeezed his hand. "But I'm okay now." He looked at her thoughtfully, his brow still furrowed with worry, but said nothing more.

When Jamey came down off the ride, they made their way toward the exhibition halls. Tom joked with her and Jamey about the sights they saw along the midway. When Jamey spied his Aunt Casey working the ladies' auxiliary booth, he ran to her, then beamed with pleasure as she praised his costume. When Casey caught sight of Dorothy she laughed heartily. "Who'd have thought you'd come dressed as the other Dorothy? Nobody can accuse you of not being a good sport, that's for sure. You and Jamey both look terrific."

"How about me?" Tom sniffed.

Casey looked him up and down critically. "So what are you supposed to be?"

"A gentleman farmer, of course."

"One out of two isn't bad, I guess. At least you wore your *good* jeans." Casey wrinkled her nose at her brother and turned her attention back to Dorothy. "Did you make the costumes yourself?"

"Yes, on the sewing machine in your old bedroom. It took me forever."

"Well, you did a fantastic job. You and I should go and check out the sewing and craft exhibits while the men look at the prize cattle in the livestock barn. I'm due for a break here anyway."

"Sounds like a great idea," Dorothy said.

Tom looked at her with feigned surprise. "What? And pass up a chance to see a bunch of prizewinning bulls? You have such a way with them and all."

"It's tempting, but I think I'll pass. Hickory might get jealous."

A grin tugged at the corners of Tom's mouth. "Whatever you say. Jamey and I will meet you back here in an hour."

Casey and Dorothy walked to the corrugated metal building beside the livestock barn, and started down a corridor lined with exhibits of fancy sewing and embroidery. One of the first displays was a hand-crocheted baby outfit, fitted onto a lovely antique porcelain doll. A blue ribbon lay beside it. "This is really nice work," Dorothy observed, reaching out to lightly touch the delicate, lacy baby cap. "It really deserves first prize."

"Thanks. Ned thinks it's too frilly for a boy, but I doubt if Junior here will object." Casey patted her belly, which had grown perceptibly in the short time since Dorothy had last seen her.

"You made this? Wow. You really are talented at needlework. I'd love to be able to do something like this," Dorothy said, genuinely impressed.

"If you like, I can show you sometime. Then you can have an outfit all ready for your first baby."

"So, I hear you're going to have a son." Tom addressed his brother-in-law Ned, who was setting a bucket of grain down for a very eager colt.

"That's what the sonogram said." A tall, lanky man with a shock of blond hair spilling over his forehead, Ned grinned broadly. "How about that, Jamey? You're going to have a cousin to play with in a couple of months."

"Yay!" Jamey beamed at his uncle and resumed stroking the colt's long, skinny neck. With Ned's permission, he'd entered the little enclosure with the colt while Tom waited outside. It nuzzled his neck, and he giggled. The livestock were being exhibited in a large barn with rows of stalls, and the colts were obviously Jamey's favorite of the show. "Can we ride this colt when he's old enough?"

"Sure. I hear you've got a new horse. Why don't you tell me about her?"

This'll take a while, Tom thought, and smiled tolerantly as his son launched into a spirited description of his new horse's virtues. As he leaned against the stall's corner post, Tom felt a tap on his shoulder.

"Hello there, Tom."

Tom turned to see Sheriff Harvey Gulch standing before him, wearing the aviator mirror sunglasses he seemed to like so much even though it was now fully dark outside.

The rows of lanterns strung overhead created a distracting glare off the amber surface of the shades, and Tom blinked involuntarily. He vowed he would not let this clown ruin his evening. "Hello, Harvey."

Gulch looked slowly left and right. "I see you don't have the girl with you. Is she still at your place, or has she found her way back to wherever it is that she belongs?"

Tom inwardly bristled at Gulch's reference to Dorothy as "the girl" but decided not to make an issue of it. He said, "She's over in the other exhibit hall, and she'll be in the costume competition later. And yes, she's still at my place. Now if you'll excuse me—"

"I heard the weirdest rumor about her the other day," Gulch continued, oblivious to Tom's obvious desire to leave. "Somebody in town told me they heard she was a princess. Of the Netherlands, I think it was. Pretty silly, huh?"

"Yeah. Silly."

"But seriously, remember that women's shelter I told you about? The one that said they would take her as soon as a space opened up? They called me just this afternoon." Gulch reached for the notebook that always protruded from the hip pocket of his uniform. He flipped through it until he saw the page he wanted, then tore it out with a flourish and handed it to Tom. "There's an opening. They're ready to take her right now, but you have to act fast. They won't hold the room for long. You'll have to call them first thing tomorrow morning if you want to get her in there."

Tom accepted the slip of paper and shoved it into the pocket of his jeans. He caught his own distorted reflection in the sheriff's sunglasses and saw that he looked just as shaken as he felt. Part of him wanted to argue with Gulch, but that would only prolong the conversation. Maybe if he pretended to go along with him, he'd leave. "Thanks," he muttered. "I'll think about it."

"Give me a call if you decide to send her, and I'll drive her to Topeka myself." The sheriff then leaned closer to Tom and whispered, "And I haven't given up on my theory. After I checked all the national crime registries, I started scouring the neighboring towns. Whenever I have to deliver a prisoner to another county or consult with another jurisdiction, I always have their officers check to see if anyone knows anything about her. I'm going to be doing that tomorrow morning, now that I think of it. One of these days, somebody I talk to will know who she is." With that, the ruddy-faced man thrust out his chest and strutted away.

As he watched the sheriff make his way down the corridor between the livestock stalls, Tom couldn't help but think how at home the sheriff would look as part of the festival's game rooster competition.

Tom removed his hat and ran a hand through his hair in frustration. Just when he and Dorothy were getting along so well, the issue of her leaving had to rear its ugly head again. Suddenly, an awful possibility occurred to him. Had Jamey heard what was said about sending Dorothy away? He looked back around to the horse enclosure, but Jamey wasn't there. "Ned! Where'd Jamey go?"

"I thought he was out there with you," said Ned, looking bewildered. "He was listening to your conversation with the sheriff for a while, and then he went out the gate. He probably just got bored and decided to wander around and come back when you'd finished talking to Harvey."

Tom looked back and forth. If Jamey had heard his conversation with the lawman, he would be distraught. He had to find him, and quickly. "Ned, I'm going to look for him. If he comes back here, keep him here. Don't let him leave."

Jamey wandered along the row of stalls, weaving blindly in and out of clusters of adults who were looking at the livestock. He clutched his fuzzy lion's tail in both hands, using it to blot the occasional tear that he could not blink back. What he'd just heard couldn't be true, it just couldn't. But when that awful Sheriff Gulch said Dorothy should go, his dad said he'd think about it. *He'd think about it.* Poor Dorothy! He had to go tell her. If only he knew where she was. When Jamey reached the door of the barn, he looked back in the direction from which he had come. His dad would be so mad at him if he wandered off on his own, but he had to warn Dorothy. After a moment's hesitation, he wandered off in the direction of the place where he'd last seen her.

A baby! Casey's words startled Dorothy a little, but she tried not to show it. Casey was looking at her carefully, as if gauging her reaction. As happy as Dorothy had been with Tom the last couple of weeks, she'd scarcely let herself so much as dream of someday having his baby. But the thought brought a warm glow to her face that she could feel to the roots of her hair. She was sure that Casey couldn't have missed it, so she might as well be honest.

"Nothing would please me more," she began haltingly, rearranging the sawdust under her left foot with the toe of her pump. "But I think talk like that is a little premature. Things are kind of up in the air right now."

"So you haven't gotten your memory back?"

"I'm afraid not."

"I hope all that gets resolved soon. And not just for your sake, but for Tom's too." Casey resumed the stroll past the exhibits with Dorothy at her side. "I still can't get over the change in him. Both he and Jamey are back to their old selves again, thanks to you."

Dorothy looked at Casey, who seemed engrossed in examining the smocking technique on a baby dress. "Tom had never talked about Margaret much," Dorothy said. Although Casey didn't mention Tom's ex-wife, Dorothy knew that she was referring to Tom's marriage and how unhappy the breakup had made him. Dorothy felt a pang of jealousy. Tom must have loved Margaret very much for his divorce to have affected him so deeply.

Casey took a deep breath and placed her hands on the small of her back, as if suddenly weary. She sighed and led Dorothy to a wooden bench next to the wall. When she'd settled herself, she said, "Margaret wanted to be the wife of a pro football star, not a farmer. But by the time the injury ended his athletic career on the last game of their senior year, they were already married and she was pregnant. I think if it wasn't for her pregnancy, she would have dumped him in a heartbeat."

"You don't sound like you were Margaret's biggest fan," Dorothy observed.

"You got that right. That woman could be so vain, she wouldn't even let Jamey call her Mom. Said it made her feel too old. Can you believe it?"

Dorothy shook her head, remembering the time she'd heard Jamey call his mother "Margaret."

"My brother did everything he could to please that woman, but nothing was good enough for her. Tom believes in forever, and he took his wedding vows seriously, even when it became clear that Margaret wasn't the kind of woman she'd led him to believe she was. He was prepared to make the marriage work no matter what. He would have done anything for her, and when his best wasn't good enough, it made him feel like a failure. I don't even think Tom loved her anymore by the time she left him, but since he's never given himself permission to fail at anything, the breakup was still very hard on him." Casey sighed. "Thank goodness all that's in the past now. And thanks to you, Tom and Jamey are happy again."

Dorothy felt her spirits rise again. He'd no longer loved Margaret by the time she'd left, according to Casey. It seemed selfish of her to revel in that information, but she couldn't help but be glad. She couldn't stand thinking of another woman as the love of Tom's life, even if she was Jamey's mother.

After looking at the remaining exhibits, the women made their way back to the booth where Dorothy had agreed to meet Tom and Jamey. The trip through the exhibit hall had only taken a half hour, so Dorothy agreed to wait with Casey. The booth contained tables of flea market items that the women's group had collected to raise funds. Casey was immediately pressed into service again, collecting money for purchases.

Dorothy sat down on one of the chairs to wait and scanned the collection of odds and ends, bric-a-brac, and just plain junk. The stuff wasn't of much interest to her, especially in her present, keyed-up state of mind, but something in a small case of jewelry caught her eye. It was an old-fashioned military medal. She went to the case, raised the lid, and lifted the medal from among the silver buttons, earrings, and rhinestone brooches. She had no idea what the medal itself signified, and the ribbon attached to it was old and a bit faded, but it reminded her of a scene in Jamey's favorite movie. He would probably love it.

"How much is this?" she asked Casey, who had finished with the last of the customers for the moment.

"Hmm. Let's say fifty cents."

Dorothy retrieved the money and dropped the medal in her purse. When Casey leaned over the front table to drop Dorothy's quarters in the cash box, she said, "Why, there's the Professor." She inclined her head toward a copse of trees past the last exhibition hall.

Dorothy followed the other woman's gaze and saw a small man smoking a pipe and leaning against a tree. He had a fringe of graying hair encircling the back and sides of his mostly bald head. A handlebar mustache stood out winglike on his upper lip. "Who is he?" Dorothy asked.

"He's a fortune teller. It looks like he's got a tent set up again this year."

"Is he any good?"

"So good he gives everyone the creeps. He's been right on all kinds of predictions."

Dorothy watched the man enter a nearby tent. Could it be true? Could that little man with the pot belly and bald pate be a genuine seer? And if he could see into the future, could he see into the past? She felt her flesh crawl with goosebumps at the possibilities. Could this be a chance to resolve things for her and Tom by finding out her identity? She felt the urge to get up and move around. She excused herself to Casey and promised that she wouldn't go far, but as soon as Casey's attention was diverted by a customer at her booth, Dorothy started walking in the direction of the fortune teller's tent, as if drawn by forces beyond her control.

Tom caught up with Jamey in the lost-and-found tent. The boy had become lost after leaving the barn, and a kindly stranger had taken him to the tent. It had taken several minutes to assure him that there was no plot to send Dorothy away. Before that, the boy had been so miserable that it had nearly broken Tom's heart to look at him.

Jamey's fear of losing Dorothy had left Tom shaken, particularly when he realized what it meant for the future. If Tom's worst fear was realized and Dorothy had to leave them when she found out who she was, then the trauma Jamey had just suffered would only have been a dress rehearsal for the real thing. The actual loss of Dorothy, so soon after his mother left, would be devastating to Jamey. And given the tenuous state of Dorothy's memory, her eventual departure from their lives was a real possibility, maybe even a probability. Tom took off his hat and ran a hand through his hair. It was one thing to risk his own heart, but another to risk his son's. What was he going to do?

Tom felt a hand on his shoulder and looked up into the face of his brother-in-law, who jerked his head in the direction of the tent's opening. "Somebody told me you two were in here," Ned said when they were out of Jamey's earshot. "Listen, a few minutes ago, Casey saw Dorothy go into that fortune teller's tent over by the exhibition halls. I'll take Jamey to Casey's booth, while you get Dorothy. Then we'll go to the costume contest. Jamey won't want to miss that. He's a cinch to win." Ned winked.

Tom went out onto the midway and saw to his consternation that it was much more crowded than it had been earlier. The lost-and-found was on the opposite side of the fairgrounds from the exhibition halls, and it would take a while to thread his way through the throngs of people to get back to Dorothy. There was no doubt in his mind why she would go to see the psychic, who was so famous in these parts for his accuracy. And he had a inexplicable feeling that he had to stop her.

Dorothy stood outside the tent in the shadow of the trees, debating with herself on whether she should enter. The fortune teller had settled onto a chair next to the table at the center of his tent and was working a crossword puzzle by the light of a bare bulb suspended over him by a dropcord. The light reflected off his head, making it nearly as shiny as the crystal ball in front of him.

Dorothy rubbed the dampness from her palms on the front of her gingham jumper and tried to think what she should do. If this man could predict the future, then telling the past must be a snap. But she had to be careful. If she told him she had no memory, he could tell her anything he chose to without fear of contradiction. But maybe if she posed the question as a challenge, a test, he would be forced to tell the truth if he could divine it. And if he could indeed solve the riddle of her identity, she'd have no need for him to predict the future. That she could do for herself, if only she knew who she was.

She took a tentative step forward, and then forced herself to the opening of the shabby little tent. He looked up from his puzzle and peered at her over thick reading glasses. "Come in. Sit down," he urged cordially, and waved her into the chair opposite him. She sat and placed a five-dollar bill on the table between them.

"Now, young lady, let's see what the future holds for you, eh?" He reached out to draw his crystal ball closer, and Dorothy put a restraining hand on his wrist.

"Not yet."

His bushy gray brows shot upward. "Oh? What else can I do for you?"

"Before you tell my future, I want to know if you're for real. I want you to tell me what my life has been like up to now."

"Want to test me, do you?" The corners of the old man's mouth turned up in a grin which looked incongruous under the prodigious mustache. "Very well. Never let it be said that I ever backed down from a test. Besides, the past is easy—I do it all the time. In fact, I have to be able to read people's memories in order to tell the future. But I'll need one of your belongings to work with—an article of jewelry perhaps, or something from your purse."

Oh no, Dorothy thought. How could he read her memories when she didn't have any? Maybe if she gave him something that belonged to her in her old life, she could still get an accurate reading, but what was there? Everything she had was new. Then she remembered that she was wearing the shoes they'd found her in after the tornado. She reached down to slip one off.

When she'd set the high-heeled pump down on the table, the seer scratched his head and said, "Hmm. Well, I guess that'll do. Now, while I hold the shoe, I want you to concentrate really hard on your past. Here goes."

If the fortune teller was counting on her help, he had his work cut out for him. Dorothy grimaced as the little man closed his eyes and ran his fingers over the shoe's dyed red snakeskin scales.

After a few seconds, the man opened one beady black eye and leveled it on her. "You're not helping," he said reproachfully. His mustache twitched.

"I know. I mean, I wanted to see if you can do it yourself."

He opened his other eye and gave her a weary look. "You *are* a tough one, aren't you? Okay, but don't expect the information to be very detailed." He closed his eyes again and resumed his shoe stroking, only slower this time. In a few moments' time, the man's face became slack, devoid of expression, and he began to moan slightly. Then, he opened both eyes and blinked, as if struggling to bring her image into focus.

"I see two lives," he began in a monotone. "With a

brief period of violence and danger in between. Both from the forces of nature and forces of human evil. You will have to choose between these two lives. But beware, for the forces of evil are not through with you yet."

Dorothy inhaled sharply, unaware that she'd been holding her breath, and an icy chill of fear rolled down her spine.

"Begin at the beginning," she said.

"Sorry! Excuse me!" Tom shouted as he bumped into a group of teenagers waiting in line to buy candy apples and Cokes. The tent was just ahead, sheltered by a cluster of trees. He stopped and leaned on one of the trees to catch his breath when he caught sight of Dorothy sitting across from the fortune teller. He made a move to charge forward into the tent, but the words of the old man stopped him with the force of a sledgehammer, and he sank back into the shadows.

"You were born into a life of wealth and privilege," the Professor began. "And before your life changed, a rich, powerful man was to make you his wife."

Twelve

"Oh, my God!" The exclamation was out of her mouth before she could stop it. She clapped her hand over her lips and stared, round-eyed, at the fortune teller.

"What's the matter?" The Professor eyed her suspiciously. "This can't possibly come as a surprise to you." The little man leaned back and blinked a few times, understanding slowly dawning on him. "You don't know who you are, do you?"

So much for strategy, Dorothy thought, and fidgeted in the metal chair. There was going to be no lying to the all-knowing Professor. "No, I don't. I don't suppose you can rub that shoe and tell me my name, can you?"

"Sorry. I wish I could help you, but I'm not so good with names." He looked genuinely apologetic, and Dorothy warmed to him a little. "Now I understand why you couldn't help me with your memories before. Amnesia victim, are you? Poor dear." He clucked his tongue sympathetically. "You're at a disadvantage here because I'm a mentalist, you see? I can't pinpoint exactly who you are and where you came from, because I'm unable to use your thoughts and memories to help me. As a result, the images I'm getting are unusually vague. Sometimes they're a little cloudy under the best of circumstances, but they're usually close enough to the mark to impress people when they turn out to be true."

"But you can tell me that I'm rich and that someone rich and powerful wanted to marry me?"

"Yes, I got the image of a mansion, servants, that sort of thing." The fortune teller grinned, immensely pleased with himself.

"And this man?" Dorothy cringed inwardly. "Did you get an image of him?"

"No, not an image. I picked up on him because right before you left your old life, he was dominating your every thought. I think I picked up on some mental energy from your old life in spite of the fact that you can't remember it."

Something outside the tent moved, and they both started. The Professor got up and waddled to the opening, looked around and returned to his chair. "Somebody was there, but I saw him walking away. It was probably someone who came for a reading but saw I was busy. I'm sure he'll come back later." He tilted his head to one side and fixed her with a kind, grandfatherly expression. "Pardon me, dear. But the news I've just given you would tickle most young women pink, and yet I can sense you're very unhappy."

Dorothy propped her elbows on the table before her and rested her chin in her hands. "It's a long story. But in a nutshell, I've formed some attachments here, and I was hoping that I'd find my old life was free from . . . entanglements, especially of a romantic nature."

The psychic puffed out his rosy cheeks, then released

a long breath that fluttered the tips of his mustache like banners in a stiff breeze. "I see your predicament."

She sighed, suddenly weary. "Listen, if I'm so all-fired rich, how come nobody's looking for me? And how did I come to leave my old life, anyway?"

"I'm afraid I can't answer the first question. As to the second, I have a definite feeling it has something to do with the evil forces I told you about earlier."

Evil. Dorothy shivered. "How did I get mixed up with evil?" She swallowed hard and continued, "Did I ever turn to a life of crime?"

The Professor reached out and patted her hand reassuringly. "I didn't see any evidence of that, child. But, to tell you the truth, I'm a little worried about your safety, and the safety of the people around you as well. If I were you, I'd leave this place, at least for a while."

The people around you. Dorothy stared at him, stunned. "Do you really think my friends and I are in danger? What did you see?"

He released her hand and clasped his own together nervously. "It was more of a feeling than anything else. But there was one clear image." His eyebrows angled closer together. "Beware of a man wearing a red bandanna."

Dorothy's heart skipped such a long beat that she wondered if it would ever start up again. Any remaining doubts she may have had about this man's accuracy disappeared in that instant. "Is there anything else I need to know?" she asked dully, as if in shock. "Like how to prevent this danger?"

The old man pursed his lips together and shook his head, his rheumy eyes filled with compassion. "I'd try to tell your future, only I'm afraid it wouldn't be any use, under the circumstances. In order to tell the future, I have to be able to read people's pasts. It was a miracle I was able to tell you anything at all about your former life since you have no memories for me to tap into."

"I understand," she said, feeling more desolate than she ever had in her life. She murmured her thanks and got up to leave.

He gave her a sorrowful look, and a rueful smile perked up the corners of his great mustache. "I have to give people bad news sometimes, and I wish it was within my power to make things all right for them. But alas, it is not, so I'm left wondering if I'm doing them more harm than good."

Dorothy managed to give him a parting smile and left the tent. The information she had just received made her heart ache and her head spin. She paused in the shadows to get her bearings and decide what to do. She couldn't begin to think about the implications of what the Professor had told her about her former life. She had to concentrate on her immediate problem—the danger that she was bringing to Tom and Jamey.

She sat down cross-legged on the grass and watched the giddy festival-goers in the distance. Only a little while ago, she'd been one of them, with Tom at her side and hardly a care in the world. Then, with no warning, all hell had broken loose. *Think!* she told herself. After a few moments, she decided that she had two options. She could tell Tom what the fortune teller had said and let him help defend her from the danger that was to come her way, or she could leave, thereby making sure that the danger never came near Tom and

Jamey. After another moment, she realized that there was only one option, and there was nothing optional about it. It was what she had to do.

Dorothy picked a yellow dandelion growing in the grass beside her and began to twirl the little blossom between her fingers. How would she convince Tom that she had to leave? If he knew she was in danger, he'd never let her go off alone. She began to shred the petals of the dandelion mercilessly, as the solution became a little clearer. He couldn't know about the danger. That was the only way. But what excuse could she give him for leaving him after they'd begun to mean so much to each other, after she'd pledged to stay with him on the farm as long as he'd let her?

She slowly spread her hands, letting what was left of the little flower fall to the grass, and her mind took her back to the night she and Tom had made love for the first time. As soon as she'd made her declaration, Tom had told her that he wouldn't hold her to it. He wanted her to feel free to change her mind if her old life turned out to be something she'd want to return to. "Before it's too late," he'd said.

Tears came to her eyes, making the festival lights swim crazily in her field of vision. The answer to her dilemma was agonizingly simple. While she could not reveal what the Professor had said about the danger, she must reveal what he'd said about the past. She had to convince Tom she was leaving him for the promise of finding her way back to her old life. It was the only way he'd let her go.

* * *

Numbly, Tom wandered the midway aimlessly. He'd meet Jamey and Dorothy at Casey's booth, but first he needed some time to recover from what he'd just heard. He was vaguely aware of people shouting greetings to him from time to time, and he managed to acknowledge them with brief nods, but he did not stop to chat. He was in a hell of a mess, and it was his own damned fault. Each time he tried to think about what he should do next, the words of that hateful fortune teller sprang into his head: In her old life, Dorothy had been engaged to a man—a rich man—who had dominated her every thought. *Her every thought.* She must have been crazy in love with the guy. A shard of pain drove its cold, jagged edge into his heart and he staggered over to one side of the sawdust-strewn path and propped himself against a light post.

Hadn't he always known there was such a man, from the time he'd seen the ring mark on her finger? Hadn't he figured out almost from the beginning that she belonged in a rich man's world? And yet, he had put not only his own heart at risk, but that of his vulnerable little boy as well. And what about Dorothy? She was the one who could be hurt the most. What had he been thinking?

He cursed himself savagely and continued on. He'd gone only a few feet before he ran headlong into a full-length mirror propped up on a stand. Springing backward a step, he looked around and saw that he was right outside the funhouse. Out from among the babble of hundreds of voices, the barker's spiel came to him with maddening clarity. "Enter the funhouse, where reality is not what it seems!"

When his gaze swung back to the mirror, he saw that his image was grossly distorted. His arms and legs seemed to go on forever, stretching out absurdly from an abbreviated torso. His eyes blinked back at him in panicky confusion from a misshapen head. Reality was not what it seemed, all right. He could write the book on that.

His whole relationship with Dorothy had been based on a fantasy. Hell, the name he called out when he made love to her wasn't even her own, but that of a character from a fairy tale. A fresh wave of pain washed over him. He drew back a fist to smash the mirror, but stopped at the last moment, forcing himself to sidestep the thing instead. He had to put a stop to the fantasy, and quickly. Because a fear even bigger than Dorothy's leaving had begun to form a tight lump in his throat. It was the fear that she would stay and grow sick and tired of life on the farm—the fear that her love for him would turn to resentment.

He'd return them both to reality, no matter how much it hurt, and he'd do it tonight.

Dorothy paced back and forth beside the booth where she'd agreed to meet Tom, sick with the anguish of knowing what she was about to do to him. Part of her wished she had taken Casey's attitude toward the Professor to heart and never gone near him, remaining blissfully unaware of the danger. But she quickly shoved the selfish thought aside. She could not repay Tom's kindness by putting the safety of him and his son at risk. She loved him too much for that.

She looked at Jamey, who was idly surveying the collection of used toys on the side table of Casey's booth. As hard as it would be to tell Tom she was leaving, she couldn't bear the thought of telling Jamey.

"Did you think I'd gotten lost?"

She spun on her heel to see Tom, who wore a strained expression. He said, "I got a little sidetracked looking at the livestock."

Casey and Ned walked up, arm-in-arm and smiling. They'd changed into costumes portraying Raggedy Ann and Andy.

"How adorable!" Dorothy enthused. "How were you able to persuade Ned to wear a costume? You can see how successful I was with Tom."

Casey laughed. "He told me he'd dress up only if I could think of a costume that would incorporate his overalls. He thought he was home free until I came up with this little brainstorm."

"Poor devil." Tom rubbed the back of his head and slid Ned a sympathetic glance. "I seem to remember being hoodwinked by a few of Casey's brainstorms in my time."

As usual, Casey ignored her brother's jibe. "C'mon, it's time for the dance, and the costume competition is coming up. I think Jamey and Dorothy are real contenders. The music's started already. What do you say?"

Jamey nodded his head so vigorously that the fringe of his lion's mane waved back and forth. The amusement Dorothy felt to see Jamey's reaction was short-lived, for when she looked up, her gaze locked with Tom's. His green eyes drilled her with a look so intense that she took a step backward. Then his black lashes fluttered once or twice and his expression changed to one of casual indifference.

"Can we, Dad?" Jamey looked up at his father hopefully.

"Sure."

Casey and Ned started toward the building where the dance was to be held, with Jamey right behind them. Tom turned to Dorothy and offered his arm. The innocent gesture seemed charged with a force that was at once irresistible and frightening. She looked up at him, but his back was to the nearest light, and a shadow cast by his Stetson obscured his eyes. Only his mouth was clearly visible, soft and sensual in the diffused light. As she reached up to take his arm, she thought she saw his lips tighten with tension.

When they entered the makeshift dance hall, the country band was in the middle of an infectious western swing tune. Tom bought Jamey a candy apple and settled him on the bleachers to watch the dancing. By that time, the band had shifted gears into the lovely, mournful Tennessee Waltz. Tom turned to her and extended his hand. She took it, and soon they were gliding across the floor among the other couples.

Tom did not make eye contact with her, but seemed to be watching the other dancers. It seemed odd to Dorothy that, after his bold display of affection on the midway, Tom was now holding her almost primly as they danced. His right hand at her waist kept her an arm's length away from him. A vocalist sang the melancholy lyrics to the waltz, something about another man taking his sweetheart away. She searched her mind for a topic of conversation to fill the awkward silence.

"While we were looking at the exhibits, Casey told me a little about what your marriage to Margaret was like."

"Why?"

She blinked at him in confusion. His voice was a degree cooler than she had ever heard it before. "So I could understand you better, of course."

He made a snorting sound and continued to stare into space. "Is that so important?"

"Yes, I think that understanding is important in any relationship." She bit her lip. Why was she preaching to him about relationships when she was about to have to break theirs off? She'd spent the time she was waiting for Tom and Jamey trying to think of a way to tell him she was leaving. But her mind had gone mercifully blank whenever she tried to think of a life without Tom.

"I've been thinking about that," Tom said hoarsely. "Our relationship, that is, and what it's based on."

"What do you mean?" She saw him swallow and avert his face from hers even more.

"It's based on a fantasy." He brought his gaze to hers for the first time since they had started dancing. "You have a real life somewhere. And you have to go out and find it, for your own sake."

Before she could say anything, he led her off the dance floor and into a corner of the building. They were near an exit, where several people had gathered for a cigarette break, and a layer of stifling smoke hung in the air.

"Here," Tom said. "I want you to look at this." He reached into the pocket of his jeans and produced a torn slip of paper covered with a childish scrawl.

She took it. There was a name, Harbor House, a

Topeka address, and the words: professional counselors. "What is this?" she asked him with confused apprehension.

"The sheriff gave it to me. It's a women's shelter. They have counselors there who can help you find out where you come from."

"You want me to leave?" Dorothy couldn't believe what she was hearing. The light was dim, and she strained to see his face more clearly through the haze of cigarette smoke.

"It's for the best. You owe it to yourself to find out who you really are. If you don't, you won't know what you could be giving up."

He did want her to leave. Grateful now for the darkness, she stared at the paper again so that she would not have to look at him. She knew she should be glad that he'd spared her the pain of being the one to end their relationship, but she never imagined that he would be the first to broach the subject of her leaving. Not after what they'd shared the last two weeks. But to hear him tell it, all that was just a fantasy—smoke and mirrors, nothing more. She took a deep breath of the fetid air and thought that she would faint, but by sheer willpower, she forced herself to be calm despite the pain that was building underneath her breastbone. The bottom line was, he was giving her a graceful way out, and she had to take it. And to think, she'd been worried about hurting him.

"The thing is," he continued, his voice low, "they only have one opening and they can't hold it for long. You'll have to call them right away."

Slowly, to keep her hands from shaking, she opened

her small shoulderbag and slipped the paper inside. "You're right, of course. I'll call them first thing in the morning." She hoped that Tom would believe her eyes were tearing from the smoke. "If you don't mind, I think I'd like to leave now."

Tom nodded curtly and took her arm to lead her back to where Jamey was, but as they reached the middle of the dance floor, the music abruptly stopped and the house lights dimmed. They'd paused to look around and see what was happening when Jamey appeared at their side and tugged at his father's sleeve.

"They're about to give out the awards for best costume," he said.

A portly man stepped onto the stage and went to the microphone. "Greetings all," he began, as a screeching burst of static reverberated from the sound system. When the noise died down, he continued. "I hope everyone is enjoying our annual Spring Corn Festival. This is the moment some of you have been waiting for. Our judges have been circulating through the crowd checking out all the terrific costumes, and I'm now ready to declare our winners."

The drummer began a slow roll on his snare drum as the announcer took a dramatic pause and waved the paper in his hand with a flourish. "Ladies and gentlemen, winners in the children's and women's categories, respectively, are—Jamey Weaver and Dorothy!"

Dorothy stood dumbly as the people around her turned to smile and applaud. She was vaguely aware of Jamey's shout and of Tom's nudging her toward the stage. Jamey took her hand and led her up the steps and toward the announcer. The applause still ringing in her ears, she accepted a small metal trophy from the stranger and watched as Jamey did the same. Blinking into the spotlight, she turned to face the crowd for a moment. An electronic flash went off somewhere in front of her, blinding her even more as she looked out over the sea of silhouettes. One stood out from the others, as tall and as still as a statue, his Stetson hat pointing strangely downward as if he were hanging his head.

As the announcer went on to call out the winner of the men's award, Dorothy took advantage of the diversion and led Jamey from the stage. Tom was there and helped them down from the risers. "Follow me," he said, pointing toward a corner exit. "Let's go out over there so we won't have to fight our way through the crowd to the entrance."

"But I want to show Aunt Casey my trophy," Jamey protested.

Tom held the door for them and ushered them out. "I'll take you over to Aunt Casey's house tomorrow and you can show it to her then."

After I've gone, Dorothy thought, and gasped for lungsful of the fresh air, which didn't make her feel one bit better.

She'd taken it awfully well. Tom stared at the ceiling, his hands clasped behind his head. He lay naked on his bed, letting the breeze from the open window caress his body. The air was too cool, but he liked its numbing effect. He only wished he had something to numb his heart as well.

No, she hadn't protested at all. In fact, she'd immediately agreed that he was right. Of course she had. She'd just been told she had a fortune and a fiancé to return to. Tom massaged his temple to try and banish the pain in his head. He supposed he should be glad she'd gone along with him without a lot of dramatics, like begging him to let her stay, or insisting that he was the man for her no matter what.

He only hoped telling Jamey she had to leave would be as easy. Fat chance of that.

Tom closed his eyes and wished that tomorrow would never come, that the earth would spin itself into some cosmic time warp that would suspend all human action for eternity.

He thought he heard something—his door moving open and then closed? The atmosphere in the room changed almost imperceptibly, and he sensed that he was not alone. He opened his eyes and saw Dorothy standing naked near the foot of his bed. At least he thought it was Dorothy. The ethereal creature looked like she was made of moonbeams rather than flesh and blood. A shaft of moonlight backlit her perfect body, bathing it in bluish illumination. Wispy tendrils of hair shone around her head like a halo. If she had sprouted gossamer wings and flown away, he would not have been surprised. She looked at him solemnly, reverently, her eyes luminous.

She crawled onto the bed on her hands and knees and suspended her body above his, so that her hair fell all around his face like a veil of satin, obscuring the moonlight and all other sensory detail not emanating from her and her alone. Her spring-rain fragrance, the feel of her skin against his, the sound of her lips nipping at his neck, all came to him more acutely than any sensations before, making him feel both weak and strong at the same time. His arms came around her as she lowered her body onto his.

"Are you real, or are you a dream?" he heard himself ask in a ragged whisper.

As she traced her lips along his collarbone, he thought he heard her murmur, "I'm just a fantasy."

Much later, propped on his side, he wound a silky curl around his finger as he watched the gentle rise and fall of her breasts. The brilliant moonlight spilled over her once more, giving her body an otherworldly glow. He ran his fingers over the alabaster skin of her throat, then tried to smooth the crease in her brow that marked a troubled sleep. His breath caught as her unconscious form followed his touch like a flower turns to the sun. She snuggled her head against him and he looked down into her face and took her in his arms for the last time.

The beautiful fantasy of the last few weeks was over. How could he ever have allowed himself to think that it would last a lifetime?

Thirteen

"I'm telling you, Luther, I don't like this place." The tall, skinny man shifted uncomfortably in the upholstered booth and cast a brooding eye over his surroundings. "Don't you know donut shops are magnets for cops just like trailer parks are magnets for tornadoes?"

His scruffy partner scowled over the rim of his coffee cup. He wasn't used to getting up this early and he was in a foul mood. "For Chrissakes, Otis, will you just chill?" Lowering his voice to a menacing whisper, he continued, "It's been weeks since we kidnapped that Spencer broad. If the cops were going to come for us, they'd have come already."

"It is pretty weird that nobody came for us when she got loose, but we've been moving around so much, maybe we've fooled 'em. Hey, maybe we just have honest faces." He took a bite of his donut, leaving a residue of white powder on his crooked nose.

Luther rolled his eyes. "Yeah, we look as innocent as little lambs. Listen, I don't know why the cops didn't come after us, but there's got to be a reason. The whole thing doesn't make sense."

The two had been on the run since the kidnapping
had gone awry. They had risen before dawn that morning to move again, skipping out on their rent.

A bell attached to the door rang merrily, signaling
that another customer had just come into the diner.
Luther, seated with his back to the door, looked up to
see Otis's eyes become as round as the saucers underneath their coffee cups. He glanced over his shoulder
to see a large policeman settle himself in the booth directly behind him, facing Otis.

When Otis did not immediately lose his deer-caught-
in-headlights stare, Luther kicked him savagely under
the table. Otis opened his mouth to cry out, but Luther
grabbed the remains of the powdered donut and stuffed
it between Otis's teeth, so that the noise he produced
was no more than a muffled groan.

While the waitress was taking the lawman's order,
Luther took another quick glance. He didn't know what
all police insignia meant, but unless he missed his
guess, this guy was a captain or maybe even a chief.
Could be Otis had been right after all. There was a first
time for everything. Still, they'd draw more attention to
themselves if they left than if they stayed put.

Otis had barely recovered from the blow to his shin
when the bell rang again and his eyes widened to their
former stricken look. Another furtive peek over his
shoulder told Luther the reason why. A second lawman,
this one wearing the tin star and brown uniform of a
sheriff, had entered and was standing next to the police
chief.

"Mind if I join you?" Luther heard the sheriff ask.
The policeman said nothing, but must have made an

affirmative gesture, because Luther felt the back of his seat quake inward as the sheriff wedged his considerable girth into the booth behind him.

Otis was still staring wide-eyed. Luther drew back his foot for another kick, but Otis reacted in time and dodged the blow. Luther's foot connected painfully with the backside of the booth, and he bit back a scream. Otis gave him a smug smile, showing more than one missing tooth. *You'll have even fewer teeth when I get you out of here,* Luther vowed silently.

"I thought I'd find you here," the sheriff said in a pompous tone. "I hear you hang out in this donut shop so much, the folks in town call it the second precinct."

Otis flashed his gap-toothed grin again, this time with I-told-you-so triumph. Luther seethed and reached down to rub his throbbing foot.

"What are you, a sheriff or a comedian? You want to tell me what you're doing in my county, Harvey?" the policeman asked.

"Got a weird missing persons case, Chief. Or maybe I should say it's a *found* persons case."

"Huh?" the chief muttered.

Otis leaned toward his partner and hissed, "Let's get out of here while they're distracting each other." He downed what remained of his coffee and wiped his mouth with the back of his hand.

Luther nodded, adjusted the greasy bandanna that held back his equally greasy hair, and fished into his jeans pocket for money.

The sheriff began speaking again. "Remember when we had that tornado several weeks ago over in Fairweather? The same day, we found a Jane Doe who

claimed she didn't know who she was because of a
bump on the head. I think she's a crook because the
Cadillac she was driving had no tag or VIN. She's staying out at the old Weaver farm for right now, but I'm
keeping my eye on her."

Luther and Otis froze simultaneously. Luther was sure
that, this time, his own eyes were just as big as Otis's.
He gestured for Otis to stay put and settled back into
his side of the booth.

"She says her memory hasn't come back, and there
are no warrants or missing persons reports out on a
woman of her description anywhere," the sheriff continued. "I'm fanning out from Fairweather into neighboring towns and counties to see if anybody knows
anything. Here's her picture. I took it just last night."

Luther heard the sound of a notebook opening and a
piece of paper being slapped down on the formica ta-
bletop. He made a grab for the check and scooted out
of the booth.

"In this get-up she looks like Judy Garland in *The
Wizard of Oz,*" the chief observed.

The sheriff made an ugly, snorting sound. "Yeah, and
guess what? She goes by the name of Dorothy. Ain't
that just the cutest thing you ever heard?"

"Never seen her before." The chief shrugged and took
a sip of coffee from the green institutional plastic cup.

Trying to look nonchalant, Luther started walking toward the cash register, with Otis on his heels. Passing
as close to the lawmen's booth as he dared, he craned
his neck to see the photograph in front of the chief.
Otis's sharp intake of breath told Luther his henchman
had seen the same thing he had.

It was the Spencer bitch. And with a few discreet inquiries, they'd know where to find her and make her pay for all the trouble she'd put them through.

He'd have to bust Otis's chops for ever being sorry they came in here. It was the best idea he had ever had.

It didn't take Dorothy long to pack her meager belongings into her makeshift suitcase, a brown paper grocery bag. If the Professor was correct, she probably had a whole set of designer luggage somewhere.

Big deal.

She took one last look around her bedroom and sighed. She'd put away the ironing board, vacuumed up every last scrap of thread, and carefully closed up the sewing machine. The room looked exactly the same as it had the first day she'd seen it, except for the little trophy sitting on the windowsill. Other than that, not a trace of her remained. On her way out the door, she cast one last longing look at the bed where she'd shared so many passionate nights with Tom and wondered what had ever made her think those nights would never end.

The door made a soft "click" behind her, and she started down the hallway to the stairs. She'd already called the women's shelter and told them to expect her later that day. She'd also put a call in to Sheriff Gulch and left the message that she would take him up on his offer to drive her to Topeka. The only thing left to do was say her good-byes. And then it would be over.

The house was as silent as a tomb, leading her to believe that Tom and his son were outside. She took a deep breath when she passed Tom's bedroom, where she'd spent one last night of ecstasy in his arms. The bed was neatly made, and there was no sign of him.

She paused at the door to Jamey's room, and was surprised to see the little boy sitting on his bed. In his chubby hands he held the trophy he'd won the night before.

"Hi," Dorothy said.

"Hi." He looked up, and she could see that he'd been crying.

She took a deep breath and sat down on the bed beside him, setting aside her grocery sack and shoulder bag. "I guess your dad told you that I have to go."

He nodded solemnly.

"And did he tell you why?"

"Yes. But I still don't understand."

How did you explain something like that to an innocent little boy whose whole world went no farther than the borders of this farm? After a moment she said, "Look closely at your trophy. See how you can see your reflection in the metal?"

Jamey peered at the polished surface of the trophy. Its rounded shape caused his image to distort. "Yes, but it's all weird. It doesn't look like me at all."

Dorothy reached out to smooth his tousled hair. "It's as if you were looking at another boy, isn't it? A stranger." When Jamey nodded she continued, "It's kind of like that when I look in the mirror. The person I see is a stranger, and now I have to go and see if I can find out who she is—who *I* am."

Jamey set down the trophy and put his arms around her, resting his head on her shoulder. "I know that you have to leave. Dad said so. And he told me I'd have to be brave, but it's really hard. I . . . I don't think I can be brave enough to say good-bye."

Dorothy's heart went out to the little boy, and she gave him a fierce hug. Sometimes words alone were not enough when reasoning with a small child. Luckily, she had one trump card. When she'd bought it the night before, she had been meaning to give it to Jamey just for fun, but now it served a more serious purpose. As she removed it from her shoulder bag, she prayed that it would work.

"You're a very brave boy, and I can prove it." Dorothy took the medal that she had bought the night before and opened the clasp. "You are now a member of the legion of bravery." She pinned the medal on the bib of his overalls.

Jamey's green eyes widened. "Wow!" He reached down and examined the medal gingerly, as if he wasn't convinced it was real.

"You have the courage to face anything, Jamey. All you have to do is believe in yourself. And if you ever forget that, well, now you have a medal to remind you."

"Thanks, Dorothy." He managed a lopsided smile that tore at her heart.

His arms went around her again and she hugged him, resting her cheek for a moment on his head, her lips grazing his silky hair. He'd been like her own child for the past few weeks. She'd played the role of his mother, and had even gone so far as to allow herself to think of him as hers. What would she ever do without him? She had to remind herself that it was for his sake that she was leaving—to protect him and his father from the danger the fortune teller had warned her of. She forced herself to gently push him from her and stood, gathering her purse and paper bag.

"I'm going to write to you as soon as I get back to my home and tell you how to reach me. I want you to know that I'll always be your friend and that you can get in touch with me whenever you want. But for now, I guess it's good-bye." She choked on her last word to him. A single tear had begun a trek down one of his round, rosy cheeks. Before her own welled-up tears could fall, she left.

Jamey sat still and listened to her footsteps until they died away. Then the front door opened and closed, and he knew that she was gone. Wasn't there something he could do to make her stay? He couldn't think of a thing.

He ran to the window and saw that Dorothy had started for the barn. Of course, she wouldn't leave without telling his dad good-bye. He still had a few minutes left to think of something to say or do, but what? He drummed his fingers on the windowsill and thought as hard as he could. Nothing. Maybe if he went out there and listened to what Dorothy and his dad said to each other, he would get an idea. He sure wasn't in any position to do anything here in the house.

He ran down the stairs and out of the house as fast as he could go. Dorothy had gone toward the big double doors, so Jamey went the other way, toward the smaller door that led to the stairs to the hayloft.

Once inside, he realized he wouldn't be able to hear them from this end of the barn, so he climbed the steps to the loft and tiptoed to the opening where his dad would throw bales of hay down to the horse and cows at feeding time.

He sneaked over to one side of the opening and flattened his back against the wall. He was right above their heads, but they couldn't see him. He crossed his stubby fingers and waited. For what, he didn't know.

When Dorothy rounded the corner, she nearly collided with Tom's wheelbarrow. They both stopped in their tracks, and Tom dropped the handles of the barrow and straightened. They both stood awkwardly for a moment, not looking at each other directly. When she finally stole a glance at him, she wished she hadn't. He was shirtless, and his muscles stood out in sharp definition from the exertion of shoveling whatever it was that filled the wheelbarrow.

"Horse manure," he said, and grasped the handle of the shovel that was poking out of the stuff in the wheelbarrow.

She started. "What?"

"I've just been mucking out Emily's stall. I was on my way to the refuse heap with the, ah . . ."

"Horse manure."

"Yeah." He placed his hands on his hips and allowed himself to look at her. His eyes looked just as hungry as hers felt. His gaze went to the grocery bag and grew even more troubled. "Hey, I meant for you to take some changes of clothes with you. You'll need them, at least for a while."

Dorothy waved a dismissive hand. "It's not necessary. Really." A sheen of perspiration covered his bronzed chest, and a tiny rivulet made its way from the hollow of his throat down into the soft curls over his breast bone. "The sheriff should be here any time, I suppose." And if he didn't get here soon, she was afraid her resolve to leave might falter, especially if she continued to look at Tom.

Tom looked toward the horizon, which was turning a threatening brownish gray. His dark brows drew together and his jaw looked taut enough to break. "I want to thank you for everything you've done for us."

Dorothy stared hard at him, trying to memorize every line of his chiseled profile. "It's me who's indebted to you. Where would I have been if you hadn't taken me in?"

Tom made a scoffing noise. "You might have been home with your family right now if I'd been more aggressive in helping you find them."

"You couldn't. You had the planting to do."

"Or maybe I just didn't want to."

He turned his wounded gaze on her and her reserve crumbled. She ran to him, but he stepped backward and put up his hands in a gesture of supplication.

"No," he rasped. "Don't. If you did, we'd both change our minds, and I can't allow that. You have to find out who you are and where you belong. You owe yourself that much. You have to go."

She opened her mouth to protest, and then remembered the real reason she was leaving. Tom didn't know about the danger, and she would keep it that way. Then, from the corner of her eye, she saw a cloud of dust forming at the end of the driveway. A cloud of dust that contained an approaching car.

"I guess this is good-bye," she said.

He nodded stiffly and studied his scuffed work boots. After a moment, he looked up again and squinted toward the driveway. "That's not the sheriff."

Dorothy followed his gaze. An old rattletrap El Camino bumped down the drive as if it had never seen a shock absorber in its long and road-weary life. The back was filled with all manner of junk, as if a dirt-poor family were moving all its worldly possessions in a single trip. Emerging out of the dust cloud as it was, it looked like something straight out of *The Grapes of Wrath.*

The car finally came to a halt and two men got out. One was tall and skinny, the other short and wiry-looking. Both were dressed in metal-studded leather so shabby no self-respecting Hell's Angel would have been caught dead in it. The short, swarthy one wore a greasy felt hat pulled halfway down over his eyes.

They made their way at a lope across the grassy lawn and came through the barnyard gate toward Tom and Dorothy. Tom stepped closer to her. "Do they look familiar?"

"I'm . . . not . . . sure." But she was. And they were. She just didn't know how or where she'd seen them, and she wasn't sure she wanted to.

"Katherine!" the shorter one said, and charged toward her, his arms outstretched. When Tom took a protective step forward, placing himself out in front of Dorothy, the other man froze, but his feral-looking smile faltered only a little. "Don't you know me, Honey? I'm Luther, your lovin' man!"

Dorothy almost swooned. "Katherine," she murmured, testing the name on her tongue. The name felt right, but the man didn't. "No, you're not. I mean, no, I don't know you. I've never seen you before." She fervently hoped it was true, rather than believed it.

The man gave her a wounded look and gestured toward the tall one. "Well, now, surely you know your brother, Otis." That one gave her a jagged smile, revealing several gaping holes where teeth should have been.

Tom gave her a sidelong look that clearly said, *No way.*

Dorothy shook her head and tried to keep her knees from shaking as well. The feeling that she'd known these men was becoming stronger. But she was absolutely certain that the last thing she should do was to go with them.

Luther clucked his tongue, cocked his head to one side, and gave her the once-over with beady eyes as black as his hat. "The sheriff told us this might happen. Said you didn't know who you were or where you came from. We've been looking for you all this time, see? And when we described you to the sheriff, he told us just where you were. So we're here to take you home, darlin'."

She looked sharply at Tom and shook her head again, this time more emphatically. With an abrupt inclination of his chin, he told her he understood.

"She's not going anywhere with you," he said evenly. "So just go on back to wherever it is you came from."

The short man cut a wary glance at Tom and shifted his weight. "Now, come with us like a good girl, and there won't be no trouble." Dorothy could see droplets of sweat begin to run down his face. Then he reached up to take off his hat, and as he did, she let out a gasp. For a headband, he wore a bandanna. A red bandanna.

As quick as a lightning strike, Tom grabbed the shovel by the handle and brandished it at the men. The little man emitted a nasty belch of laughter, and a savage gleam came into his eyes. Like a flash, he reached behind him, and when his right hand came back around, it held a large revolver, its barrel pointed straight at Tom.

She screamed as the one called Otis grabbed her, pinning her arms to her sides. "I'll go with you! Just don't hurt him!"

"Drop the shovel, plowboy," Luther snarled.

Frustration and rage written on his face, Tom did as he was told.

"We got her now, Luther! We got old Miss Rich Bitch back!"

"Damned if we ain't," Luther replied with another hoot of laughter.

"Got me back? What do you mean got me back?" Dorothy tried not to squirm against Otis lest he tighten his smothering hold on her.

"You really don't remember, do you?" said Otis, tightening his arms around her anyway until her ribs hurt. "Let's tell her, Luther. What could it hurt now?"

"Sure, why not? If Old MacDonald here plays his cards right, we might just let him live, and he can deliver our ransom demands."

"Ransom?" Tom's eyes moved from Luther to Dorothy and back again.

"That's right," said Luther, waving the gun carelessly. "The chick's an heiress. Katherine Spencer's her name.

We kidnapped her in a parking garage after some kind of shindig they threw for her at the university where she worked."

Dorothy saw spots in front of her eyes, whether from the sudden revelation of her real identity or from Otis's suffocating bear hug, she didn't know. She worked at the university—that was why the photos in Tom's yearbook had been so familiar! Even though she was being held at gunpoint by thugs, a wave of relief rushed over her—she was beginning to understand who she was!

Her gaze went quickly to Tom with a measure of relief. Luther had said he would let Tom live if he wasn't given any trouble. Surely Tom wouldn't do anything reckless, if only for Jamey's sake, but the firm set of his jaw and the menace blazing from his green eyes made her wonder. Thank God Jamey was safely up in his room.

Paralyzed with fear, Jamey stared through a knothole in the side of the barn at the bad men holding his father and Dorothy at gunpoint. He had to do something, but what? He couldn't run back to the house and call for help without being seen, and even if he could, he was so scared his knees would buckle before he'd gone ten steps. As he pressed himself closer to the wall, he felt something against his chest and looked down. It was the medal Dorothy had given him. Slowly, he reached up and stroked it. She said it would help him remember he had courage, and that was all he needed.

Jamey took a deep breath and turned around to face the inside of the loft. His father hadn't left any pitchforks up here, and there was nothing else he could see that could be used as a weapon. Then his eyes came to rest on a barrel lying on its side in a corner, and he got an idea.

He tiptoed over to the barrel and pushed against it gingerly. It was empty, so it would be easy to roll. He then started rolling it toward the opening, grateful that the layer of hay on the floor of the loft absorbed the sound.

"So that's about the size of it," Luther continued. "We'll be leaving now, and you can call that rich fiancé of hers and tell him to get together all the cash he can lay his hands on and wait for further instructions."

Tom's expression went from enraged to murderous, and a shard of fear pierced Dorothy's heart. Not only was Tom being held at bay by a creep with a very large gun, but adding insult to injury, all his worst fears about her had just been confirmed. She was every bit the rich city girl he'd been convinced she was, and she did indeed have a fiancé. As her gaze darted back and forth between Tom and the thug with the gun, she prayed all this would not be enough to put Tom over the edge.

She saw Tom narrow his eyes, and his hands flexed and fisted. The fury was still in his eyes, but a calculating look was there as well. He was looking for a weakness, an opening. *Oh, no,* she thought helplessly.

Tom stared at the greasy little cretin standing across from him. The gun was almost as big as he was, and he still waved it nonchalantly in one hand. When he fired it, he'd have to bring his other hand up to steady it. That would be the time to strike. All Tom had to do was provoke him and be ready to make his move.

"If you think for one minute that I'm going to let you take her away from this farm and disappear with her, you're as crazy as you look."

"Oh yeah?" asked Luther, his face reddening. "Well, I've waited a long time to pull a job like this. And no corn-fed farm boy is going to stop me."

Just as Tom knew he would, Luther brought his left hand up to support the gun, and as he did, Tom sprang, Dorothy's scream echoing in his ears. His shoulder connected solidly with the little man's midsection, sending Luther sprawling backwards onto the wheelbarrow of horse manure, Tom right on top of him. Tom heard a noise, and at first feared the revolver had gone off, but it was not a sharp report, but a hollow "thunk." Tom grabbed the gun, which had popped loose on the ground when he hit Luther, and stood up.

"Help me! I can't move! My leg's broke!" Luther moaned from on top of the manure pile.

Tom raised the gun and wheeled on the spot where Otis had been holding Dorothy. "Let her go!" As soon as he'd shouted the command, he saw that it was unnecessary. Both Otis and Dorothy lay on the ground, neither of them moving. A barrel lay across Otis's chest.

Jamey sat at the opening of the hayloft, his feet dangling down below him, his eyes as big as all outdoors. "Dad, I didn't mean to hit her! I just meant to hit the bad man."

"She'll be all right, son," Tom called to him as he

ran to her, wishing he knew for certain that she would, in fact, be all right. He crouched beside her, laying the gun on the ground. A trickle of blood had formed on her forehead and crept toward her eyes. "Oh please," he muttered as he put his hands beneath her shoulders and gently lifted her against his chest. "Oh, please, be all right." He pulled a clean handkerchief from his back pocket and pressed it to her wound, applying firm, steady pressure.

He hugged her to him fiercely and prayed as he had never prayed before. *Let her be all right. If you let her be okay, I promise I'll make sure she does what's best for her. I won't be selfish and try to keep her here, not that she'd want to stay anyway. Just please let her be okay.*

He rocked her gently in his arms until he felt her stir. Then he leaned his head back and looked down into her eyes. "Are you all right, Dorothy?" At first he saw on her face a dull questioning look, but as he stared deeply into her eyes, they slowly lit up with comprehension. In that split second, he felt a keen awareness that something was different. "Or should I say . . . Katherine?"

"Yes," she breathed. "I'm Katherine."

Fourteen

Tom paced the hallway outside Katherine's hospital room, waiting for the doctors to finish their examinations. So much had happened in the last few hours, he could hardly take it all in. Seconds after Katherine and Otis had been hit on the head, Sheriff Gulch had shown up. Both of the crooks had to be taken to the hospital; Otis had a probable concussion, and Luther almost certainly did have a broken leg. Served the bastard right, Tom thought. He'd have all the recuperation time he needed in the state prison.

Jamey had been pretty wired at first, but had calmed down when he realized Dorothy—that was, Katherine—wasn't badly hurt. After the ambulance left with her, Tom had dropped him off at Casey's on the way to the hospital. They had been putting Katherine through a battery of neurological tests, and Tom hadn't had as much as a glimpse of her since he'd arrived. He longed to see her, although he had no idea what he'd say to her when he did. She was a different person now, not his Dorothy at all. He'd really lost her, he thought, letting his suddenly weary body sag against the wall.

He'd managed to flag down a nurse who told him that Katherine's memory was coming back slowly, and that she was still confused about most aspects of her former life. But physically, she would be just fine. He was grateful for some good news for a change. Everything else he'd learned about her today had been awful. And the really fun part hadn't even begun yet. The shadowy man whose existence had been the stuff of his nightmares, the man who would take Katherine from him, was about to get a name and a face.

He had righted himself again and pivoted on his boot heel to walk back down the green-tiled corridor he'd just traveled for the hundredth time when he caught sight of Sheriff Gulch coming toward him. The sheriff looked red-faced and frazzled. It had probably been the most exciting day on the job that Harvey ever had in his life.

"There you are," the sheriff said breathlessly. "How is she?"

Gulch took a wary step backward as Tom narrowed his eyes on him, weeks of pent-up resentment bubbling to the surface. "Oh, sure. You're concerned about her now that you know she's *somebody.*"

"Now, Tom, that's not fair." Gulch began haltingly. "You have to admit I was almost right about her. I mean, she *was* involved with the crooks I was looking for, only instead of being their accomplice, she was their victim."

Tom shook his head. Only the sheriff's twisted logic could take a situation where he was dead wrong and make it sound like he was "almost right." Still, there was nothing to be accomplished by taking out his frustration on the man, no matter how tempting it was. Tom stared at the ceiling tiles and leaned back against the cinder block wall. "I suppose you got in touch with her family."

The sheriff removed his hat and scratched his stubbly head. "She doesn't have any family, actually. Her parents are dead, and she doesn't have any brothers or sisters. But I did manage to contact her staff—"

"She has a *staff?*" Tom asked weakly. Of course she did. He'd known she would have people working for her. Rich girls usually did.

"Yes," Harvey went on. "From what I understand, she's a very wealthy woman." His eyebrows went up and down for emphasis. "Oh, and I also contacted her fiancé."

Tom felt his teeth grate at the sound of the word *fiancé*. "I suppose he's on his way."

"Yeah." The sheriff looked at his watch. "Should be here anytime. I filled him in on everything and told him I'd meet him here."

Tom leaned his head back, letting it make harder contact with the wall than he meant to. After everything that had happened today, beating his head against the wall felt good. "I'm sure he'll appreciate it."

"Hey, I'll bet that's him now." Gulch pointed toward the hospital's helipad, which was visible from the double glass doors leading to the back parking lot. The pad was usually used by the county's rescue copter, but the one easing toward earth now was a sleek corporate model. The thunderous *thump, thump, thump* of its rotor was the most ominous sound Tom had ever heard. He winced as he saw the skids touch the ground.

"Wow! That's some whirlybird. And I'll bet it belongs to Mr. Richards. That's Michael Richards of Richards Mining." Sheriff Gulch leaned toward Tom for emphasis.

Tom stared grimly at the gleaming silver and black machine. "I wouldn't be a bit surprised." Too bad Kansas was landlocked, he thought. The guy could have floated up on his yacht. Tom vaguely remembered a newspaper series he'd followed about Richards Mining a few years ago. Some farming interests upstate had come up against some mining interests over a pending piece of state legislation. The mining interests had won. Surprise, surprise.

The sheriff struck off toward the doors at a full waddle, jamming his hat back on as he went. Tom maintained his position outside Katherine's room like a sentry, his arms crossed tightly over his chest, his eyes on the helipad. A man alighted from the copter, and Tom's mouth dropped open in surprise. If this was Katherine's fiancé, she had a taste for older men. The man was tall and thin, and his hair, being furiously whipped about by the rotor, was snow-white. Right behind the man was a woman about his age, dressed in a white uniform.

Strange, Tom thought. And then, as the third person climbed down from the copter, Tom's back stiffened and the hairs at the nape of his neck stood up. That was him, Michael Richards. Tall and blond, Richards closed the distance between the helipad and the hospital in long, athletic strides. He ducked slightly as he walked and covered his head with his hand, no doubt to keep the wind from mussing his hair. He wore a suit that looked custom-tailored and expensive even at a distance.

Sheriff Gulch had attached himself at the hip to the man by the time he reached the walkway. Good thing there were double doors, Tom thought. By the time the party had reached Katherine's hospital room, one of her doctors had stepped out into the hallway, and the introductions were made. The older man and woman were Mr. and Mrs. Finch, Katherine's groom and cook, respectively. They stood, arms linked, concern etching their faces.

"And this, Mr. Richards," Sheriff Gulch began, his chest puffed out like an overfed guppy, "is Tom Weaver. He's the man who's been taking care of Miss Spencer for the past several weeks."

Richards extended his hand to Tom and offered up a broad smile. "Tom, I can't thank you enough for taking care of my Katherine. I assure you you'll be reimbursed for any expenses you've incurred."

She's not your Katherine. She's my Dorothy. Tom shook the man's hand mechanically. He could feel his face burning with resentment and frustration. "That won't be necessary."

Briskly, Richards turned to the doctor. "Can I see her now?"

"Yes," said the neurologist. "But don't add to her stress level. She's trying very hard to remember her former life, so give her time to do that without putting any undue pressure on her. She's suffered a bump on the head, but it's nothing that won't heal easily. As to her state of mind, she's confused right now. Her memory seems to be coming back bit by bit, but it may never come back completely. She's pretty agitated, so when you talk to her, just be patient. Don't expect her to remember everything all at once."

Richards, who appeared to be concentrating intently on the doctor's words, thanked the man and was ushered into the room, leaving Tom, the Finches, and the sheriff standing in the hallway. Tom had never felt so helpless in his life, watching another man step into the role of Katherine's protector. Since there didn't seem to be anything he could do for Katherine, he might as well see what he could do for her friends. "There's a little waiting room down the hall. Why don't we sit for a while?" he suggested.

The Finches smiled gratefully at Tom and followed him to the waiting room where he bought them sodas from the machine. Tom seated himself across from them and studied their earnest, worried faces. "She's going to be fine," he assured them.

"Thank God," Mrs. Finch said, accepting the soda Tom offered. "We were so worried."

"She's been like a daughter to us since her parents were killed," Mr. Finch explained. "When we found out she was in trouble, we just couldn't believe it. We're still in shock."

"I have to ask," Tom began gently. "It's been weeks since Katherine was found without a memory. Why didn't anyone come looking for her?"

Mrs. Finch looked anguished. "We thought she was on some tropical island somewhere enjoying her vacation—having the time of her life. She was scheduled to leave right after a bon voyage party her friends were throwing for her at the university medical center. From what we've pieced together, she was kidnapped right after the party, before she'd had a chance to get to the airport."

Tom nodded, remembering what the kidnappers had said as they were trying to take Katherine away with them.

"It was a little unusual for her not to call us, but we figured she was so busy with vacation activities, it just slipped her mind." Mrs. Finch took a sip of her drink and seemed to calm down some.

"We should have known." Mr. Finch shook his head. "She's always been such a good girl, so thoughtful and responsible, we should've known that when we didn't hear from her, something had gone wrong."

"But when she left, all she said was, 'see you in September,'" Mrs. Finch said with a sigh.

"Don't blame yourselves," Tom said, patting the older woman's hand. "There's no way you could have known that Katherine was in trouble. The important thing is that you've got her back now." *And I've lost her,* Tom thought, a pang of pain shooting through his chest.

The Finches both looked at him with gratitude and visibly relaxed. "Thank you so much for taking care of her and protecting her when we couldn't."

Even though Dorothy's fiancé gave him the creeps, Tom found himself liking the Finches very much. He was glad she had them in her life. "You mentioned that she worked at the university medical center. I'm curious, what does she do for a living?"

"Well, she doesn't really to do anything for a living," Mr. Finch explained. "Her parents left her so much money she could live a life of leisure if she wanted.

But she's always wanted to help people. That's why she became a child psychologist. That and the fact that she loves kids, of course."

Tom had to smile. That explained why she was so good with Jamey. After listening to the Finches, he realized that there was so much more he wanted to know about Katherine. He leaned forward, propping his forearms on his knees. "Tell me all about her. Tell me about Katherine."

Michael Richards stepped into the hospital room, heedless of the nurse and technician who were bustling out. "Darling!" he said, spreading his arms wide but making no immediate move to come to her.

This is déjà vu all over again, thought Katherine, defensively pulling the sheet higher on her chest. She shuddered, remembering Luther's use of the endearment. Little bits of her memory had begun to return, but her old life was still mostly shrouded in fog, including the man standing before her.

"I'm your fiancé, Michael." His voice oozed sympathy. "Don't you know me, sweetheart?" He finally came to sit on the bed next to her and took her hand. His touch was cool and dry. She sensed an odd wariness about him.

She shook her head and looked at him apprehensively.

"Do you remember anything about . . . anything that happened right before you were kidnapped?"

She shook her head again. What was this man getting at? "Why do you ask?"

The man visibly relaxed and flashed a smile that reminded her of a young Robert Redford. Why could she remember Robert Redford and she couldn't remember this guy?

"I was just curious. Don't worry. You'll be home and back to your old self in no time." He squeezed her hand, not unpleasantly.

Home. She thought of the farm and then of Tom and Jamey, and her throat constricted. Then she thought of the other thing the man had said. "What is my old self? I mean, what do I do, for example? I didn't just sit on a chaise somewhere eating bonbons and reading *Town & Country,* did I?"

Michael laughed heartily at that. "Good Lord, no. Why, you're only the most prominent child psychologist in the state of Kansas."

She felt another jolt of familiarity, the most pleasant one so far. No wonder she had such a rapport with Jamey! "Was I really competent?" She felt her hope rising.

"Competent? Darling!" He flashed her another mega-watt smile. "You're at the top of your profession, widely published in the journals, staggeringly successful."

Katherine began to laugh, hugging her knees to her chest. She was good at something! Something important. Her mind flashed back to all the mishaps she'd been involved in at the farm—the near poisonings, appliance explosions, sewing disasters. How devastating they'd seemed at the time. But now they seemed so trivial.

"Of course you'll have to cut down on your work schedule after we're married."

"What?" Startled out of her reverie, her former wariness returned.

He reached into his pocket and withdrew a small velvet box. "Thank goodness this was out being appraised when you were abducted. Those ruffians probably would have pawned it immediately, and they'd have no idea of its value." He raised her hand and placed a huge diamond engagement ring on her third finger.

She stared at the stone as if mesmerized. It was big all right. It was also gauche, gaudy, and perfectly awful.

"It's a beauty, isn't it? Well, I have some calls I have to make, so I guess I'll let Matty and Jacob come in and help you get ready to go."

"Go? Go where?" She felt as if she were in a dense fog. Her old life was trying to break through the surface of her consciousness, and her head hurt with the effort.

"Home, of course," he said breezily, and stepped out the door. "Where you belong."

She squeezed her eyes shut and raised her hands to massage her temples. When she did so, her left hand felt leaden with the weight of the tasteless ring. Although her spirits had been momentarily buoyed by the talk of her life's work, she had to admit that on a personal level, the vibes she had gotten from Michael weren't much warmer that those she'd gotten from Luther and Otis. But surely that was just her imagination. She had been about to marry this man. They had to have loved each other, hadn't they?

With her eyes still tightly closed, the image of Tom appeared in her mind, his eyes full of love for her, need for her. But was she really the one he needed? Or someone who could sew a straight seam, repair a vacuum cleaner, and cook a meal that he wouldn't be afraid to eat? Sure, she had proven that she was game for these things, but she wasn't really good at them. What she was good at was helping little children who needed her more than Tom evidently did.

Even before the barn dance, Tom must have already come to the conclusion that she should leave, or he never would have gone along so readily with sending her to the women's shelter. She tried to remember his exact words when he told her she had to leave, but her new head injury had made the conversations of last night a little fuzzy. All she remembered were his last words on the subject that morning before all hell had broken loose. *You have to go.*

So, she would go. And she wouldn't sacrifice what little dignity she had by begging him to let her stay, although that was exactly what her heart told her to do.

But if he gave her the slightest opening, the barest hint that he'd changed his mind and wanted her to stay, then she knew that she would plant her pumps on the Weaver farm and stay there for the rest of her life.

Tom crushed the soda can into a jagged wad of aluminum without realizing what he was doing until the metal began to dig into his hand. Richards had just waltzed in, tersely told the Finches to see to Dorothy and then immediately got on his cell phone to see to his business matters, as if what was taking place here at the hospital was just a time-wasting inconvenience. Harvey Gulch was still hanging around, no doubt waiting to sneak in a few obsequious comments before

Richards left. Tom tossed the soda can into a metal trash can, enjoying the loud twanging sound it made. Richards, still on the phone, cut him a disapproving look. Tom smiled maliciously back at him and left the waiting room.

As he walked back to Katherine's room, he reflected on what the Finches had just told him. He felt a pang of guilt, remembering when he'd chided Katherine about her wealthy background. Her fortune notwithstanding, her life had been anything but fortunate. Born to indifferent parents, she was in and out of boarding schools and orphaned at an early age. The Finches had become her *de facto* parents, and had raised her as their own, as much as was possible for servants.

Tom's hand went to his chest where a lump had formed. It had come to him almost immediately that it was the images of Matty and Jacob that had appeared to Katherine when her memory had first tried to return. No wonder. The old family retainers were all she had.

Except for Michael Richards.

He didn't believe he'd ever hated anyone on sight before, but that was exactly what had happened this afternoon. Despite Richards's designer suit, he seemed to Tom almost as slimy as Luther and Otis. Still, she must have loved him. She had chosen him out of what must have been, Tom figured, dozens of men who had to have wanted her. After all her childhood loneliness and heartbreak, she deserved a happy, secure, carefree life. Michael Richards could give her that.

He rubbed his chest again, but the pain just wouldn't go away. He knew it never would.

Matty and Jacob came out of the room and stood on

either side of him. Matty put a gentle, maternal hand on his arm. "She wants to see you."

Tom nodded, took a deep breath, and entered the room. Katherine was sitting on the bed in the jeans and T-shirt she'd been wearing earlier today. Her head was bandaged but other than that she looked fine. Her paper bag and purse sat beside her. She was ready to go home. She regarded him with a hyper-alertness he found unsettling. She probably just wanted to memorize the way he looked so she could remember her spring fling as a pleasant diversion in years to come.

Tom cleared his throat, feeling suddenly awkward in the presence of this woman, every inch of whose body he knew like the back of his hand. "How're you feeling?"

"Great. My memory is still a little fuzzy, though. Not only of my former life, but of what happened last night and this morning too." She tilted her head forward, a gesture that looked oddly inquisitive.

"Maybe that's for the best." Tom thought about their ordeal of being held at gunpoint. It would take a person a long time to recover mentally from an assault like that.

She looked at him hard and inhaled sharply. After a moment she said, "Maybe you're right."

Tom traced a square of green linoleum with the toe of his boot. Was there a chance, just the ghost of a chance that she would keep the promise she'd made on their first night together and stay with him? Was there anything he could say to make her stay? He'd made a solemn promise to God that he wouldn't beg her to stay with him, but right now he felt as if he might give up his very soul and do just that.

He raised his gaze from the floor and saw something that froze his heart. On her left hand, which rested on her knee, she wore the biggest diamond engagement ring he'd ever seen. The missing ring was back. She'd made her decision.

"I guess this is good-bye, huh?" His own voice sounded foreign in his ears.

"Guess so." Her back stiffened and she stood.

Tom knew it was time to leave, but he couldn't bring himself to. "The first time I ever spoke to you was here in this hospital, and now I'm saying good-bye to you here. I think it may have been in this very room." Tom made a sweeping gesture with his hand. "Funny how sometimes things come full circle," he said, thinking it anything but funny.

"Yeah. I guess so." Katherine bit her lip, and her long lashes blinked a few times. "Tom," she began, and her voice trailed off.

"Yes?"

"Nothing."

He heard voices in the hallway outside and knew it was time. Walking toward her like a man in a trance, he encircled her in his arms. She returned his embrace, resting her head on his chest, right above his heart. Could she hear it breaking? he wondered absurdly. He felt her body shudder as she drew in a ragged breath. "Thank you," he heard himself say. "For everything."

"Tell Jamey good-bye for me," she whispered.

Richards walked briskly into the room. "Come along now, sweetheart."

Tom released her without meeting her eyes. She picked up her things and followed her fiancé out of the room. She did not look back.

Tom sat down heavily on the bed, feeling as empty as the sterile, impersonal hospital room, and just as cold. For a moment there, he'd almost allowed himself to imagine that she would stay with him. So many weeks ago he'd released her from her promise to stay with him as long as he would let her. Today, he'd wanted to beg her to stay, even though he'd promised God he wouldn't. Her remembered love for Richards must have been stronger than her love for him.

He looked at the pillow, put out his hand and ran it over the smooth cotton case that still bore the impression of her head. *I hope your old home is a happy one, Dorothy.* His and his son's home, unfortunately, would never be the same again.

The dream was over.

Fifteen

Weeks later, Katherine sat in her spacious office in the Spencer clinic with case files, notes and forms strewn across the desk in front of her. As soon as she'd resumed her practice, she'd remembered how much she loved working with the children. She couldn't, however, remember how she ever dealt with all this paperwork.

She rested her head on the back of her cushy leather desk chair and closed her eyes. Either memories or the lack of them had been the bane of her existence these past several months. Why couldn't she just remember what she wanted to remember and forget what she wanted to forget?

She opened her eyes again and her gaze came to rest on a small, framed photograph tucked among some other bric-a-brac on her floor-to-ceiling bookshelves. Speaking of what she wanted to forget. A guttural growl came from her throat as she sprang from her chair and stood on tiptoe to reach the picture. She thought she had purged her office and her home of any reminder of Michael Richards and their engagement. The photo showed the two of them at a party more than a year ago. She held the picture over the trash can with her left hand and dropped it in, frame and all, as she raised her right hand in a mock salute.

Good riddance to bad rubbish.

Her memory of her life and work had continued to come back after she returned to it. It hadn't taken her long to remember having broken up with Michael before she was kidnapped. His story about the ring having been out for appraisal at the time was a bald-faced lie. She'd given it back to him the very night she was abducted. He just decided to go out on a limb and bet the farm that she wouldn't remember breaking up with him and what an arrogant, two-timing jerk he'd been. Thank goodness she had remembered, just in time.

Bet the farm? Oh, no. *The farm.* She collapsed back into the chair and covered her eyes. Would she ever reach the point where every little thing didn't remind her of Tom? She still missed him and Jamey so desperately that she could hardly breathe when she thought of them.

Katherine rummaged in a desk drawer for aspirin in order to quell a budding headache. She found the aspirin and popped it into her mouth before she realized her water glass was empty. "Yurgl," she said, chewing the bitter pill. She swallowed hard, the acidy pill burning the back of her throat.

Sighing, she sifted through the mail in her "in" basket until a handwritten envelope caught her attention. Her heart thudded as she glanced at the return address. It was from Jamey! She'd been skittish about calling the farm since she left, but she made good on her promise to let him know how to get in touch with her.

She'd sent him a picture postcard of the university so that he could see where she worked. She'd also written a brief note saying she was fine and included her address and phone number. Since he hadn't started school yet, she knew Tom would have to read it for Jamey. She'd allowed herself to hope that Tom would get in touch with her himself, but the handwriting on the envelope was decidedly feminine. Her spirits plummeted. Had Tom replaced her already? And if so, was the new woman in his life the new housekeeper/nanny, or was she something more? She tore the envelope open as fast as she could.

> Dear Katherine,
>
> It seems so weird to call you that. You'll always be Dorothy to me. Aunt Casey is helping me write this letter. Thank you for your post card. The place you work is pretty. Do you miss us? We miss you. Dad doesn't say so, but I know he's real sad since you left. Won't you come for a visit? Just tap those ruby slippers together and say, "There's no place like home."
>
> Your friend, Jamey.
>
> P.S. Aunt Casey says hello and she hopes she'll see you soon.

A crudely drawn crayon picture of a pair of red pumps decorated the bottom of the note.

Katherine heaved a sigh of relief that it had been Casey who'd written the note for Jamey. She stood and went to the window, her mind reeling. Tom was hurting, but why? He had been very clear on the subject of her leaving. She massaged her forehead with one hand. The man was a master at hiding his feelings. Had he been trying to hide something when he said good-bye at the hospital?

If only she could remember exactly what he'd said the night of the dance, or the next morning before the bad guys had come. She still only remembered clearly his last words at the barn: *You have to go.*

She rested her hands on the windowsill and leaned forward, letting the summer sun bathe her. She looked down and noticed that the mark on her left ring finger was almost completely gone now.

Absently, she rubbed the fingers of her left hand. The ring mark had led Tom to suspect there had been a man in her old life, and of course he'd been right. The fortune teller had confirmed that the night of the dance. He had said she was wealthy and had been about to marry a rich, powerful man who dominated her every thought.

He dominated my every thought, all right. I was obsessed with coming up with a graceful way to dump him.

Katherine went back to her chair, sat down, and put her feet up. Tom had also been right about her being wealthy. He'd been convinced that, like Margaret, she would never be happy on the farm on a long-term basis. Maybe he'd gone along with the plan to put her in the women's shelter so the counselors could help her find her home, thinking that would literally save her life. She hadn't tried to convince him that her place was with him because she was so concerned with the danger she'd put Tom and Jamey in.

If she could only remember. Perhaps he'd even told her he was sending her away for her own sake. And then when Michael had come and taken possession of her, maybe he'd assumed it was too late.

But was it too late? Too late to change Tom's mind? Was there anything she could do now to get him to agree to take her back?

This was all too complicated. She hung her head in confusion. When she did, the labels on the case files came into focus, each bearing the name of a child who needed her. If she tried to work things out with Tom, what about the children? If he took her back, was there a way she could continue her work in such a rural, isolated area?

She let her head rest on the desk, and soon she was drifting off into a dream of a pleasant journey back to a magical place.

Tom dried his hands on a dish towel and tossed it on the counter. It was almost noon, morning chores were over, and she should have been here, bustling around making lunch. And yet the kitchen was empty and quiet.

Jamey shuffled in as Tom put a leftover tuna casserole in the microwave. "Chores done?" Tom asked.

Jamey nodded and got a soda from the refrigerator.

"How're the pigs?"

"Fine."

Tom sighed. His son wasn't very talkative these days. Jamey hadn't bounced back from Katherine's leaving any more than he had. It seemed like there were little reminders of her everywhere. Jamey had to feed seven of the little reminders every day. The pigs she'd delivered were half grown now, and were in danger of being turned into pets by Jamey, something Tom had to discourage for obvious reasons.

"You're not getting too attached to Glinda's pigs, are you?" Tom joined his son at the kitchen table. "You know, it doesn't pay to get too close to the ones who are eventually going to have to go."

Jamey looked up at him with eyes so like his own. "I guess it's the same way with people sometimes, huh?"

Tom clasped his hands together on the table in front of him and drew in a deep breath. He hadn't talked to Jamey a great deal about Katherine's leaving. It wasn't that he didn't want to comfort his son. He just didn't know what to say. "I guess you could say that, son. But that doesn't mean that you shouldn't let yourself care about people and get close to them. Dorothy—I mean Katherine—had a life somewhere else. And when she found out what it was, she had to go back to it, that's all."

Jamey took a gulp of soda and looked up at Tom. "She could have stayed here if she'd wanted to, couldn't she? Didn't she know that, Dad?"

It was a question he'd been asking himself lately. Tom was grateful that the microwave timer went off at that moment so he wouldn't have to answer it. Because the answer was, he didn't know. He'd told himself time and again that after what they'd meant to each other, surely she'd realized that she had the option to stay. But he'd practically pushed her to leave because he thought it was the best for her. And by now, she was probably

Mrs. Michael Richards. What would have happened if he'd fought for her? He spooned soupy noodles and tuna onto a plate for Jamey and slopped some over the side.

"Easy, Dad." Jamey accepted the plate and began to eat without enthusiasm.

Tom joined his son and twirled a forkful of noodles absently. He hadn't spoken to her since she left. What harm would a phone call do? There was nothing wrong with catching up with an old friend, was there? He'd be able to tell by her voice if she was happy, and if she was he'd wish her well and leave her alone. But if she wasn't . . . Hell, if she wasn't happy, she'd have gotten in touch with him by now. He dropped his fork onto his plate in disgust. He was grasping at straws.

"It's not that bad," Jamey offered. "Put some hot sauce in it."

Katherine stood on the porch, her fist poised to knock on the kitchen door, her nerves faltering. The weeks of preparation and negotiation she'd spent making possible her return to Tom were about to pay off—or not. During that time she'd debated with herself on the best way to confront him. She decided not to do what she did at the hospital—waiting for him to give her a sign had been a disaster. No, this time she would take the initiative. Crossing her fingers behind her, she knocked on the door.

Tom flung the door open and looked at her wide-eyed, clearly stunned. Jamey squeezed out past him and caught her in a bear hug.

"Dorothy! You came!"

Not taking his eyes from her face, Tom backed up to let her inside the door. Laughing, she stepped in, dragging Jamey with her.

"It's good to see you," Tom said. He stepped toward her, lifting his arms as if he meant to hug her, but Jamey still stood between them. He jammed both hands through his hair instead, looking her up and down as if he'd never seen a woman before.

"Likewise, I'm sure."

"Ah, what are you doing here?"

She noted with satisfaction that Tom's breath was coming hard and fast and a tentative smile was forming on his handsome face. "Jamey invited me. Didn't he tell you?"

Tom stared dumbly at her for a moment. "Um, no, but I'm awfully glad he did."

"I had business in the area anyway. I've been checking out the facilities of the radio station here," she said as calmly as she could. "So since I was in the neighborhood, I thought I'd stop by."

Tom blinked a couple of times. "Radio station facilities?"

"I'm thinking of producing my own radio call-in show. That way I'd be able to reach a lot more children and their parents than I can in my practice."

Understanding finally dawned in his eyes, and he took a step closer to her. "And how did you find the Fairweather radio facilities?"

"Perfectly adequate." She swallowed hard. His obvious state of shock made it hard to gauge his reaction. It was time to quit teasing and get down to business. "Tom, why did you tell me to go?"

He looked at her as if she'd cut him. "I didn't want to. Please believe me. But when I heard what the fortune teller said about your life and your fiancé . . ."

Katherine's hand fluttered to her throat. "That was you outside the tent that night!"

"Yes. I did it for you, don't you see? I never wanted you to go."

For the first time, she let her eyes betray her feelings, because she sensed victory was within her grasp. She allowed herself a head-to-toe appraisal of the powerful body and beautiful masculine face she'd missed so much.

She extended her hand to Tom, as if she wanted to shake. But it was her left hand. He took it in his own, understanding immediately. When he saw that her fingers were bare, he brought her hand to his lips and his astonished, hopeful emerald gaze to her face.

"You didn't marry him," Tom said hoarsely. It was a statement rather than a question.

"I didn't marry him."

"Why?"

"Because I love someone else."

Slowly, he began to draw her closer. "What about your other life, your servants?"

"My other life wasn't worth a plug nickel without you and Jamey. And as far as the servants are concerned, Jacob has always wanted to work on a farm, and Matty misses taking care of a real family. When you get a chance to taste it, I think you'll agree that her cooking is a shade better than mine. I thought the little cottage would be perfect for them."

"What cottage?" Tom blinked.

"The one I'm going to build for them about half a mile from here."

"Oh. *That* cottage."

"So, do you think you'd like to take on a boarder again?"

"A boarder?" The corners of his mouth began to ascend into a dazzling smile.

"I'm not much of a housekeeper or cook," she said finally, "but I try real hard, and I'm good with kids."

"Yay!" Jamey, who'd been standing in round-eyed silence, shouted and began to dance an excited little jig.

Tom pulled her to his chest and encircled her waist with his brawny, possessive arms. Then he began to laugh, and the rich, rumbling sound filled the kitchen with its warmth. His hands slid up her back and wove themselves through her hair, bringing her face to his. Between kisses, he said, "Welcome home. I love you."

After a few moments, they both looked down at Jamey, who was tugging at their sleeves and grinning. "Do I have to call you Katherine, or can I keep calling you Dorothy?"

Tom leaned his head back, his face a picture of pure joy. "If I have anything to say about it, very soon now, you'll be calling her Mom."

"I'd be honored, Jamey," Katherine said, tears of happiness welling in her eyes. "And I'll tell you something else. There's no place like home!"

BOOK YOUR PLACE ON OUR WEBSITE AND MAKE THE READING CONNECTION!

We've created a customized website just for our very special readers, where you can get the inside scoop on everything that's going on with Zebra, Pinnacle and Kensington books.

When you come online, you'll have the exciting opportunity to:

- View covers of upcoming books

- Read sample chapters

- Learn about our future publishing schedule (listed by publication month *and author*)

- Find out when your favorite authors will be visiting a city near you

- Search for and order backlist books from our online catalog

- Check out author bios and background information

- Send e-mail to your favorite authors

- Meet the Kensington staff online

- Join us in weekly chats with authors, readers and other guests

- Get writing guidelines

- AND MUCH MORE!

**Visit our website at
http://www.zebrabooks.com**